A LUCKY LUKE ADVENTURE

LUCKY LUKE VERSUS THE PINKERTONS

ACHDÉ, PENNAC
& BENACQUISTA
IN THE STYLE OF MORRIS

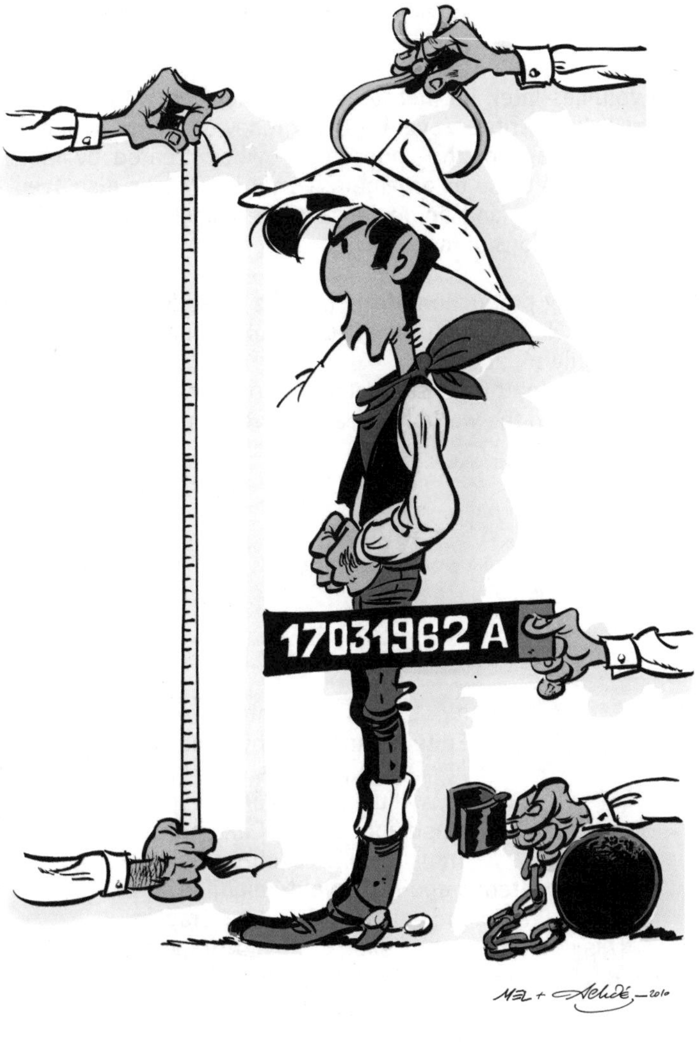
17031962 A

COLOUR WORK: ANNE-MARIE DUCASSE

9th CINEBOOK
The 9th Art Publisher

*

Morris, a genius of the ninth art!

The father of Lucky Luke was born in 1923 in Kortrijk, Belgium. After starting out in cartoon studios, he created Lucky Luke, his world and the main characters of the series, whose first adventures would appear in 1947 in *L'Almanach de Spirou*. For several years, Morris plied his trade in the United States with his friends André Franquin and Joseph Gillain and the stars of the satirical *Mad* magazine, Kurtzman, Davis and Wood; meanwhile, Lucky Luke quickly found its place in the world of comics thanks to its simple design, its expressiveness and the instincts of its creator. In fact, Morris's way with words brought forth the now-famous phrases "The man who shoots faster than his shadow" and "the ninth art."

Ten volumes later, he met René Goscinny, who would become Lucky Luke's writer. Several others followed in his footsteps. Today, the saga of the Lonesome Cowboy created by Morris encompasses close to 90 albums. Early on, Morris displayed a passion for film and animation, and he closely monitored the many adaptations of his work.

It was during production of the final 52 episodes of the series, titled "The New Adventures of Lucky Luke," that Morris passed away on July 16, 2001.
He remains one of the superstars of comic book creators. His characters and the world he created have become eternal.

* Cartoon of Morris by the artist himself

Original title: Lucky Luke contre Pinkerton
Original edition: © Dargaud Editeur Paris 2010 by Benacquista, Pennac & Achdé
© Lucky Comics
www.lucky-luke.com
English translation: © 2011 Cinebook Ltd
Translator: Erica Jeffrey
Lettering and text layout: Imadjinn sarl
Printed in Spain by Just Colour Graphic
This edition first published in Great Britain in 2011 by
Cinebook Ltd - 56 Beech Avenue - Canterbury, Kent - CT4 7TA
www.cinebook.com
A CIP catalogue record for this book
is available from the British Library
ISBN 978-1-84918-098-6

9th CINEBOOK
The 9th Art Publisher

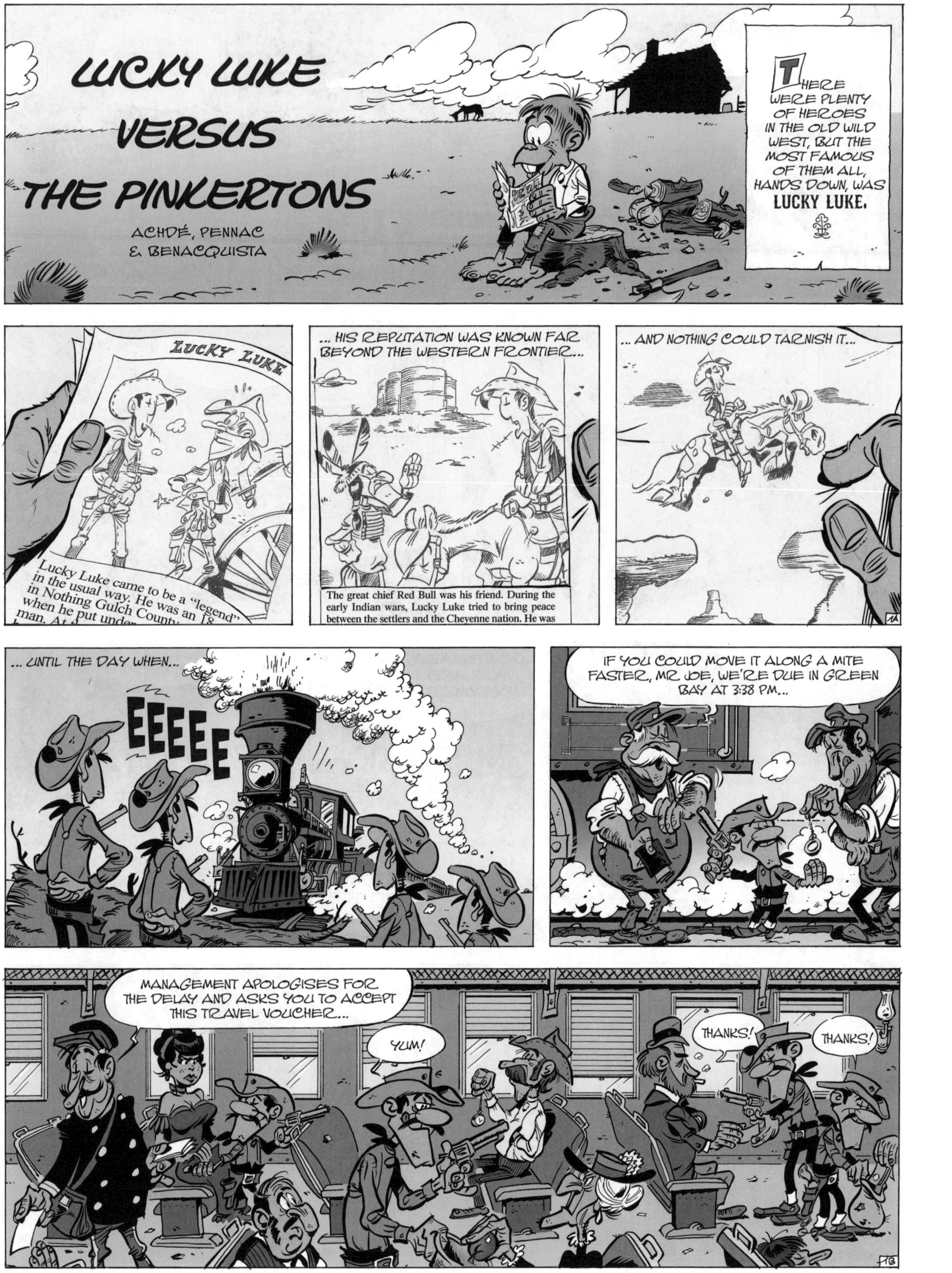
LUCKY LUKE
VERSUS
THE PINKERTONS
ACHDÉ, PENNAC
& BENACQUISTA
THERE WERE PLENTY OF HEROES IN THE OLD WILD WEST, BUT THE MOST FAMOUS OF THEM ALL, HANDS DOWN, WAS LUCKY LUKE.
LUCKY LUKE
Lucky Luke came to be a "legend" in the usual way. He was an 18
in Nothing Gulch County
when he put under
man.
... HIS REPUTATION WAS KNOWN FAR BEYOND THE WESTERN FRONTIER...
The great chief Red Bull was his friend. During the early Indian wars, Lucky Luke tried to bring peace between the settlers and the Cheyenne nation. He was
... AND NOTHING COULD TARNISH IT...
... UNTIL THE DAY WHEN...
EEEEE
IF YOU COULD MOVE IT ALONG A MITE FASTER, MR JOE, WE'RE DUE IN GREEN BAY AT 3:38 PM...
MANAGEMENT APOLOGISES FOR THE DELAY AND ASKS YOU TO ACCEPT THIS TRAVEL VOUCHER...
YUM!
THANKS!
THANKS!

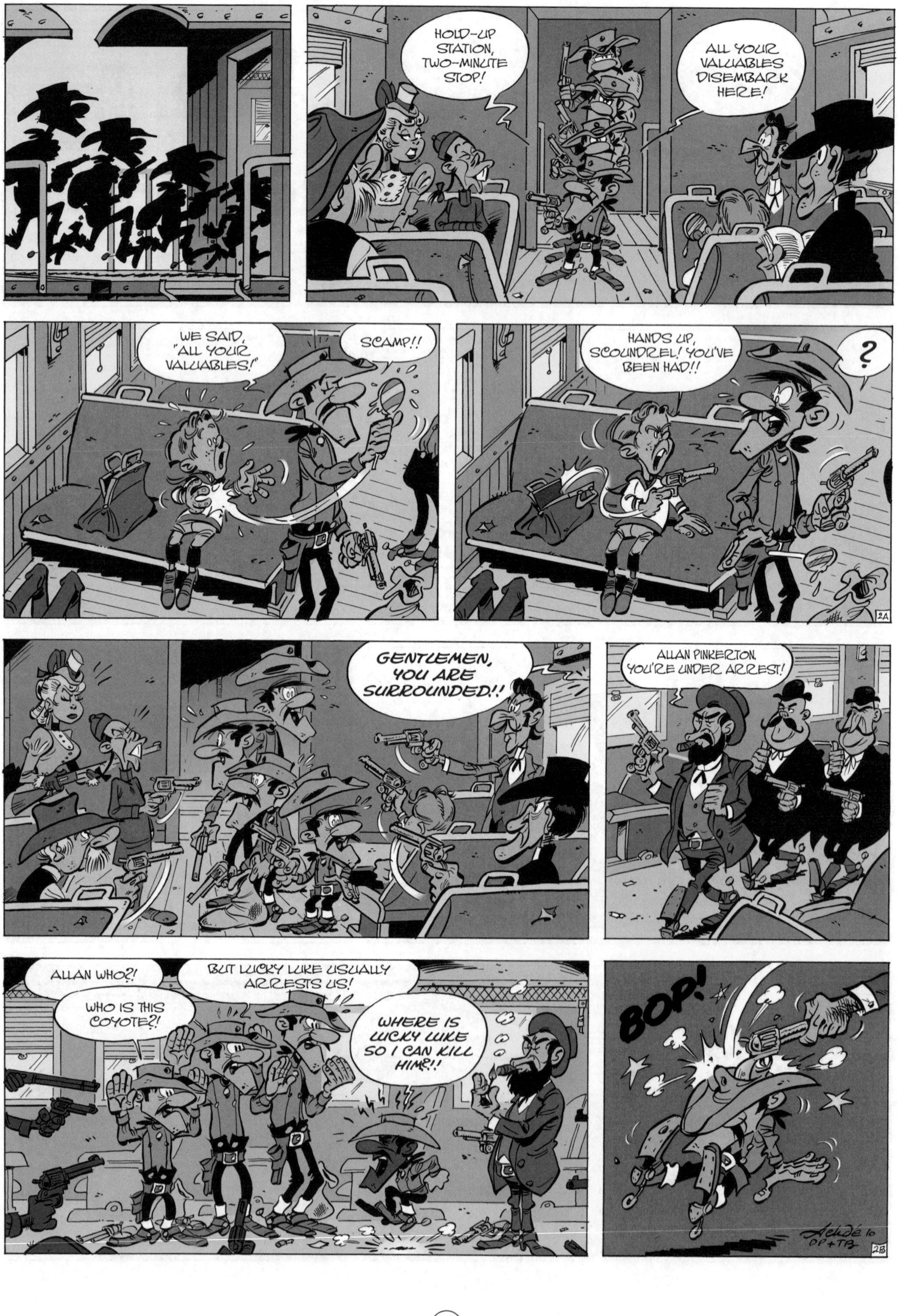

HOLD-UP STATION, TWO-MINUTE STOP!
ALL YOUR VALUABLES DISEMBARK HERE!
WE SAID, "ALL YOUR VALUABLES!"
SCAMP!!
HANDS UP, SCOUNDREL! YOU'VE BEEN HAD!!
?
GENTLEMEN, YOU ARE SURROUNDED!!
ALLAN PINKERTON. YOU'RE UNDER ARREST!
ALLAN WHO?!
BUT LUCKY LUKE USUALLY ARRESTS US!
WHO IS THIS COYOTE?!
WHERE IS LUCKY LUKE SO I CAN KILL HIM?!!
BOP!

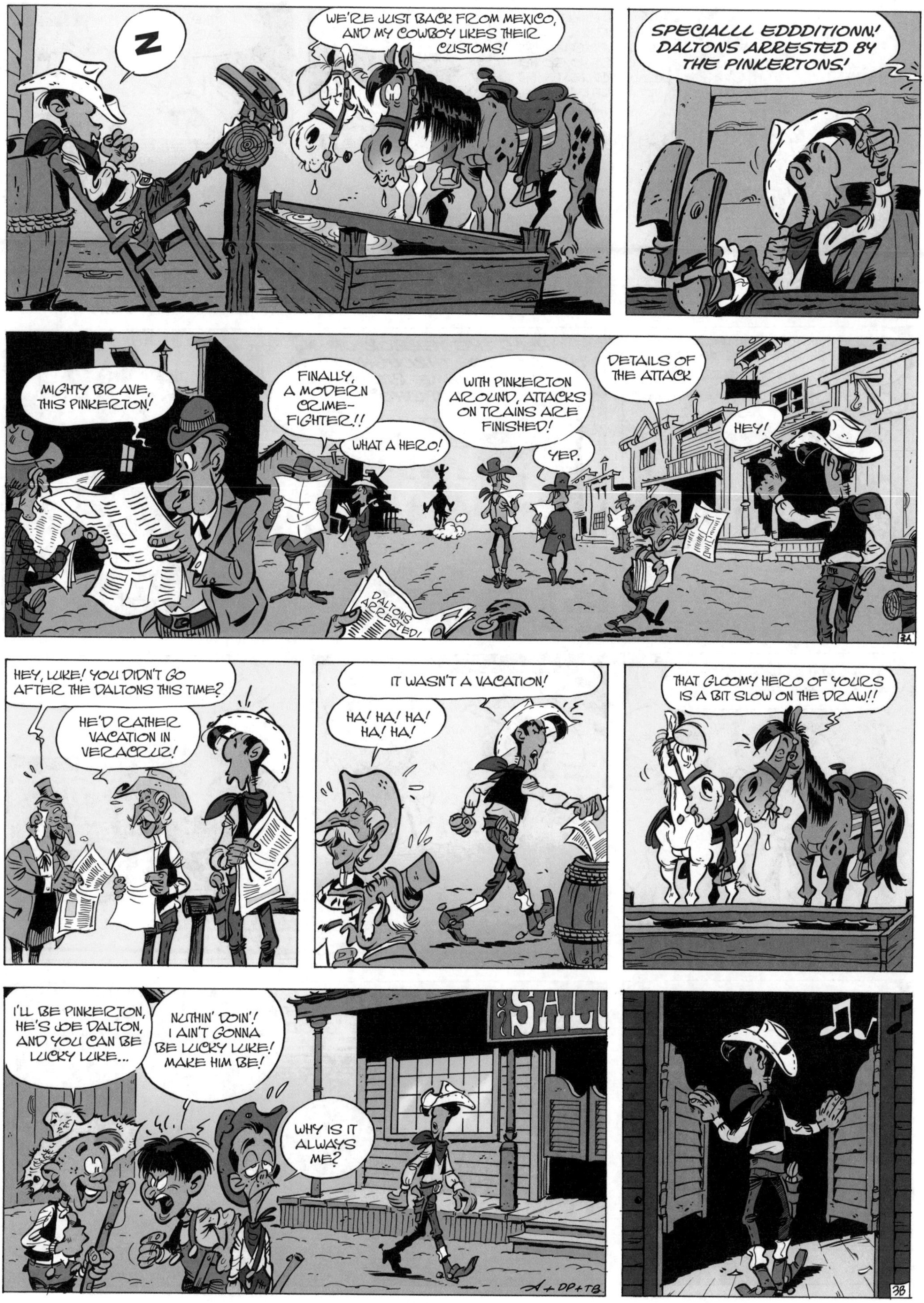
Z
WE'RE JUST BACK FROM MEXICO, AND MY COWBOY LIKES THEIR CUSTOMS!
SPECIALLL EDDDITIONN! DALTONS ARRESTED BY THE PINKERTONS!
MIGHTY BRAVE, THIS PINKERTON!
FINALLY, A MODERN CRIME-FIGHTER!!
WHAT A HERO!
WITH PINKERTON AROUND, ATTACKS ON TRAINS ARE FINISHED!
YEP.
DETAILS OF THE ATTACK
HEY!
DALTONS ARRESTED!
HEY, LUKE! YOU DIDN'T GO AFTER THE DALTONS THIS TIME?
HE'D RATHER VACATION IN VERACRUZ!
IT WASN'T A VACATION!
HA! HA! HA! HA! HA!
THAT GLOOMY HERO OF YOURS IS A BIT SLOW ON THE DRAW!!
I'LL BE PINKERTON, HE'S JOE DALTON, AND YOU CAN BE LUCKY LUKE...
NUTHIN' DOIN'! I AIN'T GONNA BE LUCKY LUKE! MAKE HIM BE!
WHY IS IT ALWAYS ME?

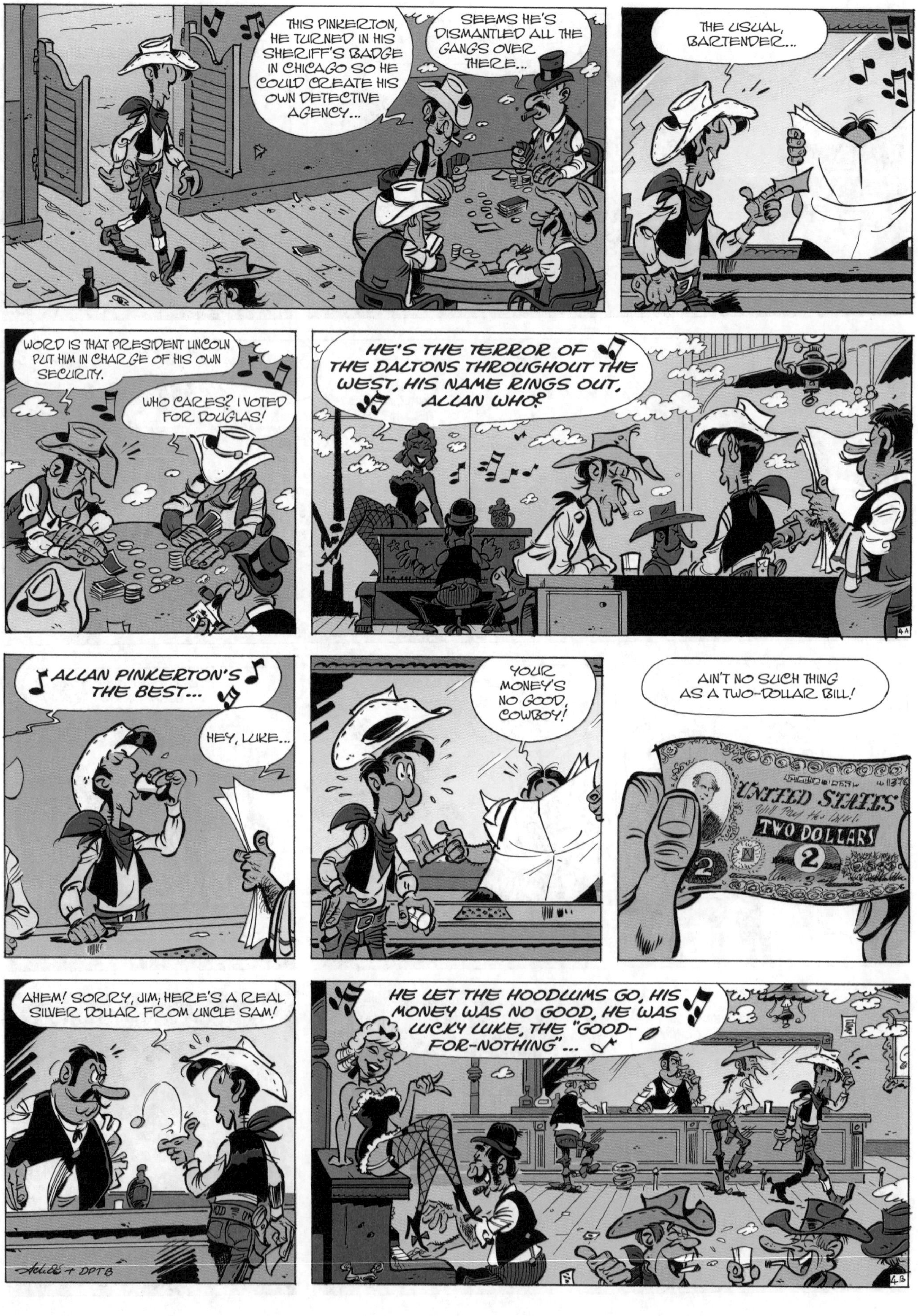
THIS PINKERTON, HE TURNED IN HIS SHERIFF'S BADGE IN CHICAGO SO HE COULD CREATE HIS OWN DETECTIVE AGENCY...
SEEMS HE'S DISMANTLED ALL THE GANGS OVER THERE...
THE USUAL, BARTENDER...
WORD IS THAT PRESIDENT LINCOLN PUT HIM IN CHARGE OF HIS OWN SECURITY.
WHO CARES? I VOTED FOR DOUGLAS!
HE'S THE TERROR OF THE DALTONS THROUGHOUT THE WEST, HIS NAME RINGS OUT, ALLAN WHO?
4A
ALLAN PINKERTON'S THE BEST...
HEY, LUKE...
YOUR MONEY'S NO GOOD, COWBOY!
AIN'T NO SUCH THING AS A TWO-DOLLAR BILL!
UNITED STATES
TWO DOLLARS
2
AHEM! SORRY, JIM; HERE'S A REAL SILVER DOLLAR FROM UNCLE SAM!
HE LET THE HOODLUMS GO, HIS MONEY WAS NO GOOD, HE WAS LUCKY LUKE, THE "GOOD-FOR-NOTHING"...
Achdé + DPTB
4B

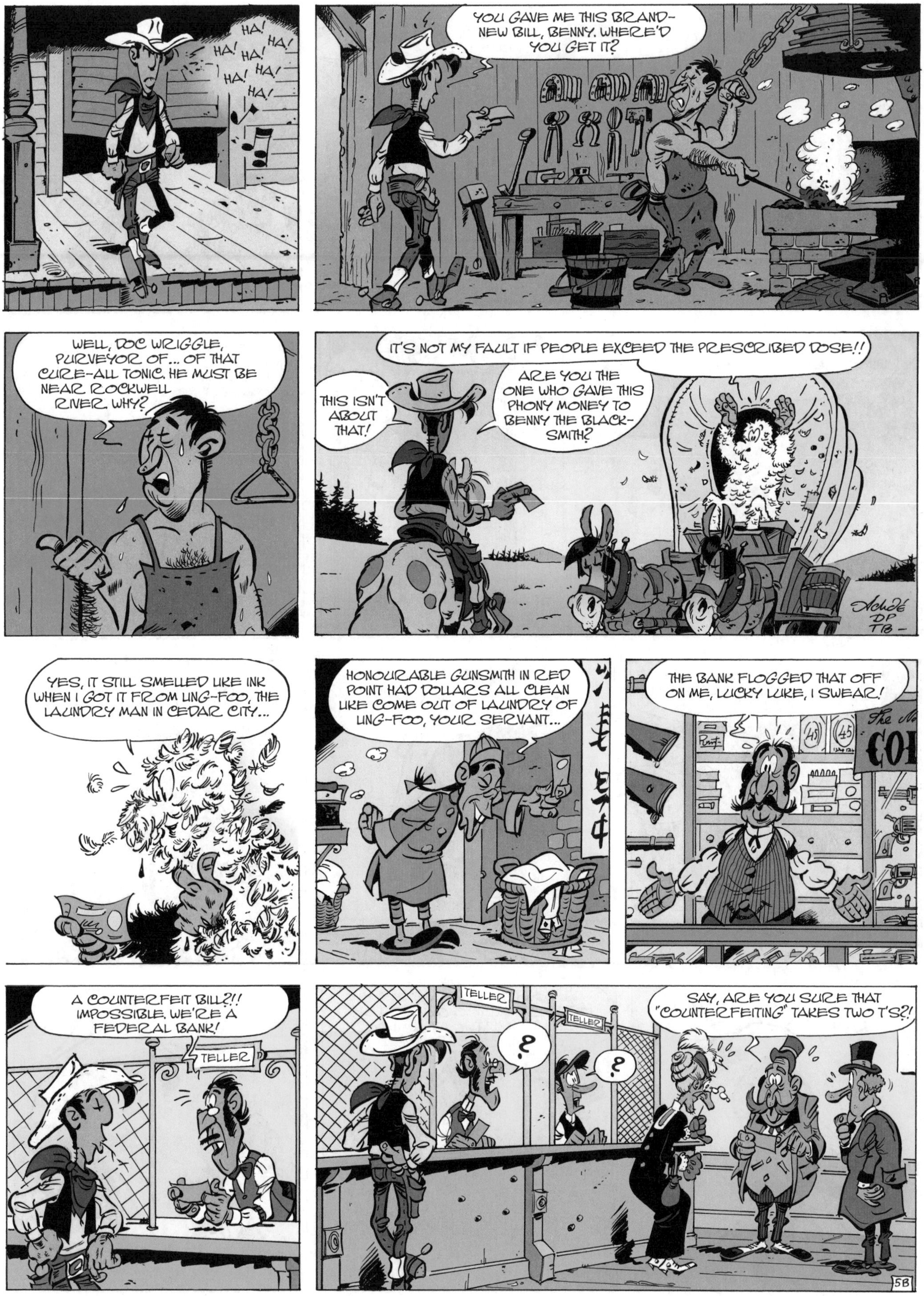
HA! HA! HA! HA! HA! HA!
YOU GAVE ME THIS BRAND-NEW BILL, BENNY. WHERE'D YOU GET IT?
WELL, DOC WRIGGLE, PURVEYOR OF... OF THAT CURE-ALL TONIC. HE MUST BE NEAR ROCKWELL RIVER. WHY?
IT'S NOT MY FAULT IF PEOPLE EXCEED THE PRESCRIBED DOSE!!
THIS ISN'T ABOUT THAT!
ARE YOU THE ONE WHO GAVE THIS PHONY MONEY TO BENNY THE BLACK-SMITH?
YES, IT STILL SMELLED LIKE INK WHEN I GOT IT FROM LING-FOO, THE LAUNDRY MAN IN CEDAR CITY...
HONOURABLE GUNSMITH IN RED POINT HAD DOLLARS ALL CLEAN LIKE COME OUT OF LAUNDRY OF LING-FOO, YOUR SERVANT...
THE BANK FLOGGED THAT OFF ON ME, LUCKY LUKE, I SWEAR!
A COUNTERFEIT BILL?!! IMPOSSIBLE. WE'RE A FEDERAL BANK!
TELLER
TELLER
TELLER
?
?
SAY, ARE YOU SURE THAT "COUNTERFEITING" TAKES TWO T'S?!

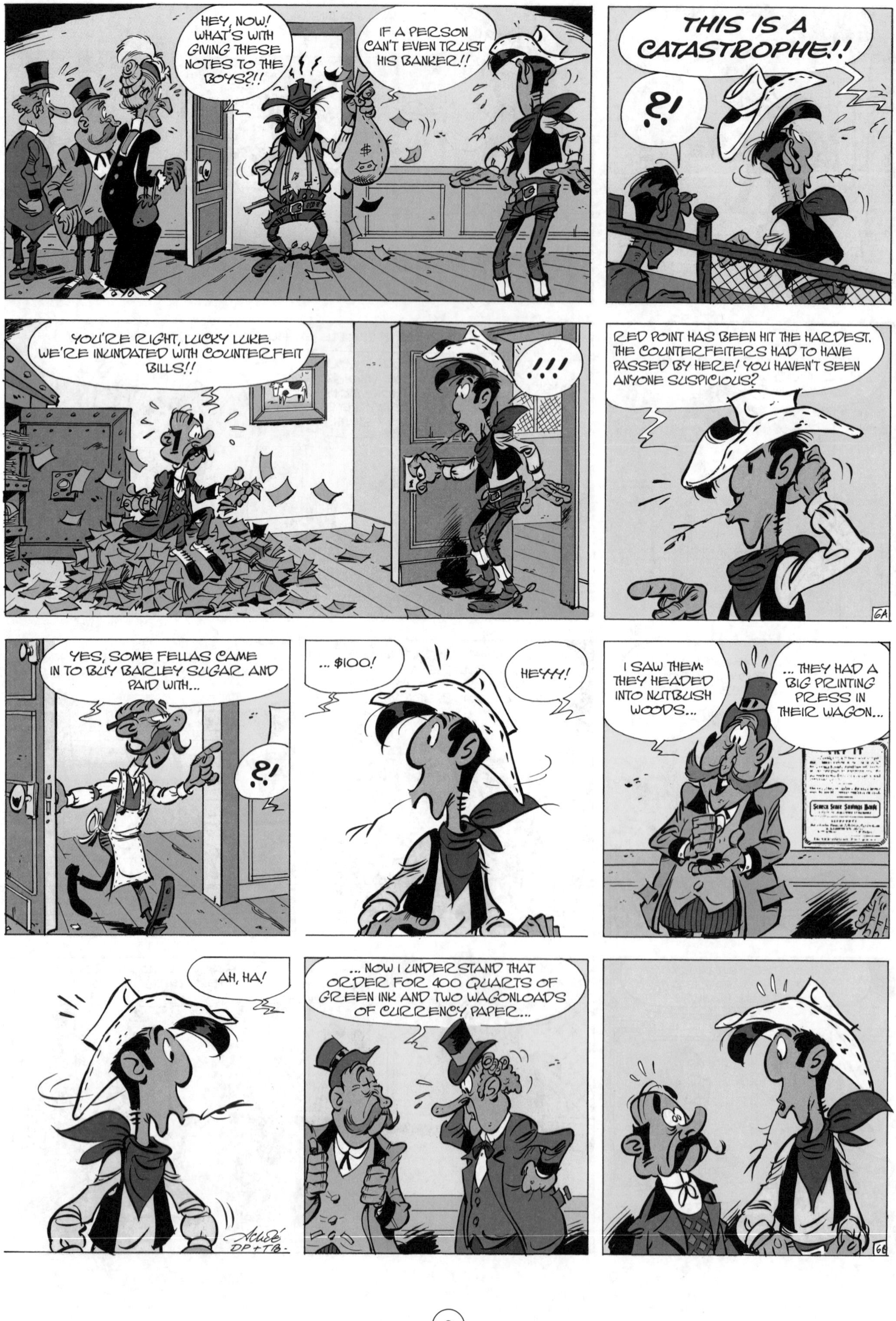
HEY, NOW! WHAT'S WITH GIVING THESE NOTES TO THE BOYS?!!
IF A PERSON CAN'T EVEN TRUST HIS BANKER!!
THIS IS A CATASTROPHE!!
?!
YOU'RE RIGHT, LUCKY LUKE. WE'RE INUNDATED WITH COUNTERFEIT BILLS!!
!!!
RED POINT HAS BEEN HIT THE HARDEST. THE COUNTERFEITERS HAD TO HAVE PASSED BY HERE! YOU HAVEN'T SEEN ANYONE SUSPICIOUS?
YES, SOME FELLAS CAME IN TO BUY BARLEY SUGAR AND PAID WITH...
?!
... $100!
HEYYY!
I SAW THEM: THEY HEADED INTO NUTBUSH WOODS...
... THEY HAD A BIG PRINTING PRESS IN THEIR WAGON...
AH, HA!
... NOW I UNDERSTAND THAT ORDER FOR 400 QUARTS OF GREEN INK AND TWO WAGONLOADS OF CURRENCY PAPER...

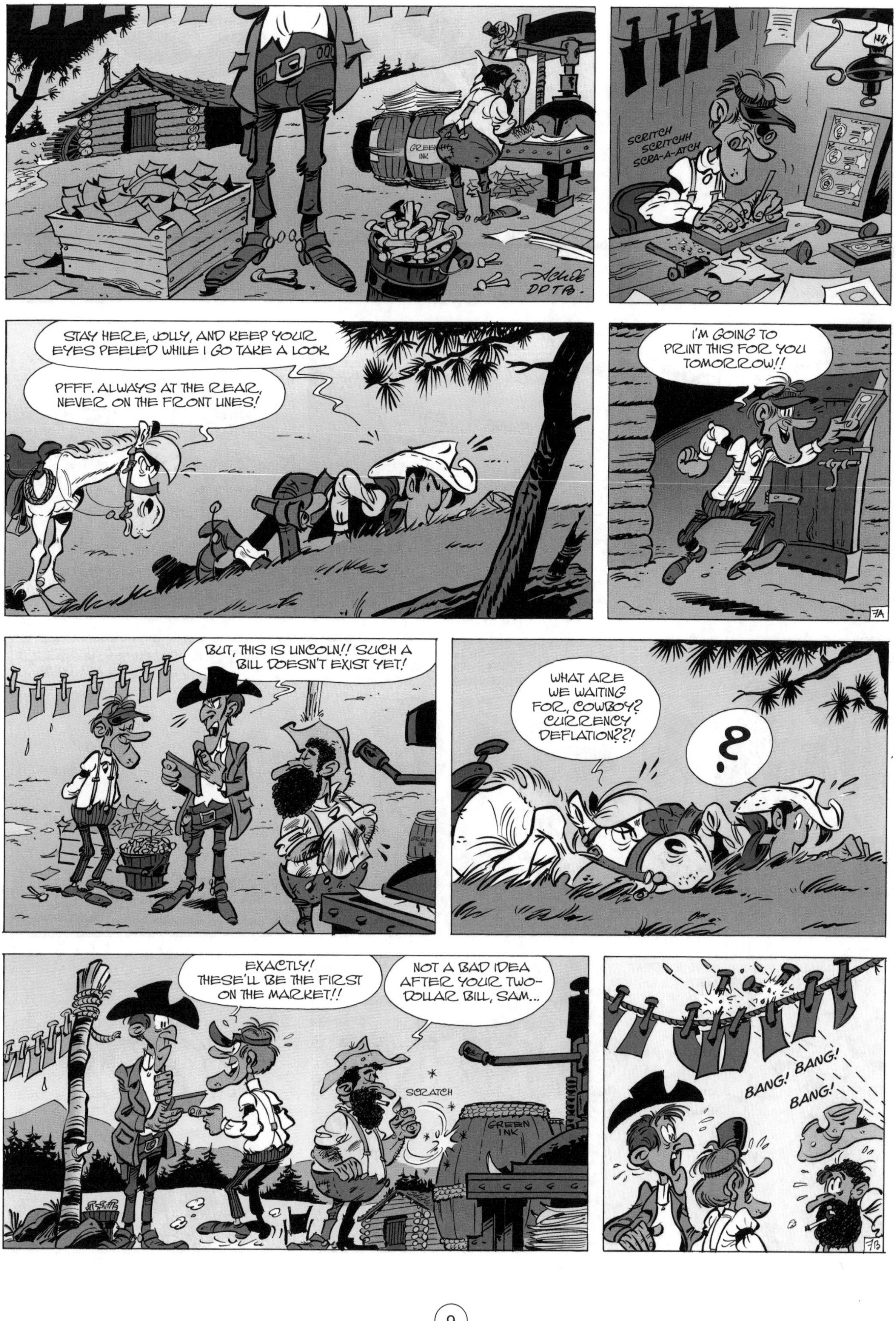
GREEN INK
SCRITCH SCRITCHH SCRA-A-ATCH
STAY HERE, JOLLY, AND KEEP YOUR EYES PEELED WHILE I GO TAKE A LOOK.
PFFF. ALWAYS AT THE REAR, NEVER ON THE FRONT LINES!
I'M GOING TO PRINT THIS FOR YOU TOMORROW!!
BUT, THIS IS LINCOLN!! SUCH A BILL DOESN'T EXIST YET!
WHAT ARE WE WAITING FOR, COWBOY? CURRENCY DEFLATION??!
?
EXACTLY! THESE'LL BE THE FIRST ON THE MARKET!!
NOT A BAD IDEA AFTER YOUR TWO-DOLLAR BILL, SAM...
SCRATCH
GREEN INK
BANG! BANG!
BANG!

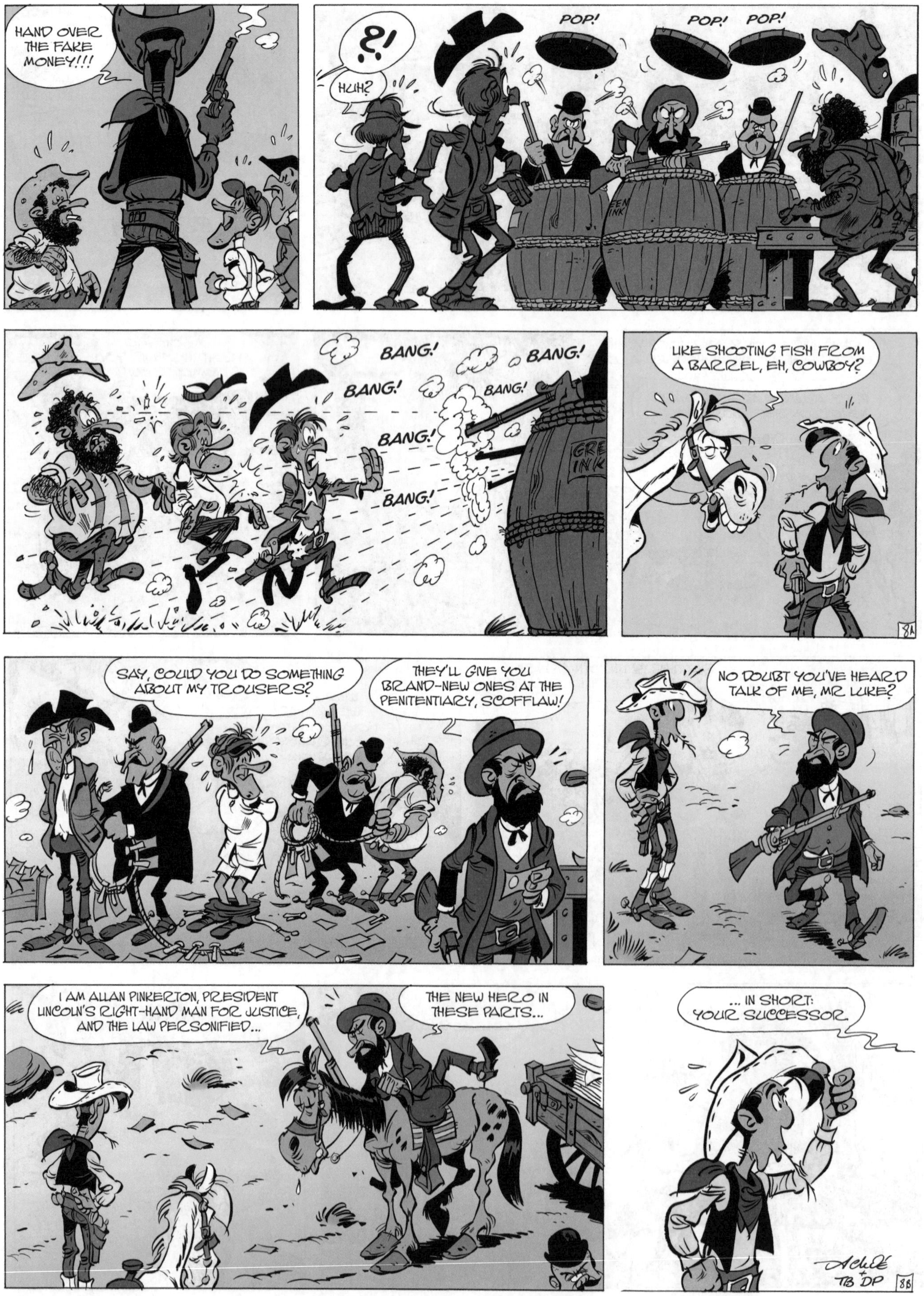
HAND OVER THE FAKE MONEY!!!
?!
HUH?
POP!
POP! POP!
BANG!
BANG!
BANG!
BANG!
BANG!
BANG!
LIKE SHOOTING FISH FROM A BARREL, EH, COWBOY?
SAY, COULD YOU DO SOMETHING ABOUT MY TROUSERS?
THEY'LL GIVE YOU BRAND-NEW ONES AT THE PENITENTIARY, SCOFFLAW!
NO DOUBT YOU'VE HEARD TALK OF ME, MR LUKE?
I AM ALLAN PINKERTON, PRESIDENT LINCOLN'S RIGHT-HAND MAN FOR JUSTICE, AND THE LAW PERSONIFIED...
THE NEW HERO IN THESE PARTS...
... IN SHORT: YOUR SUCCESSOR.
ACHDÉ + TB DP

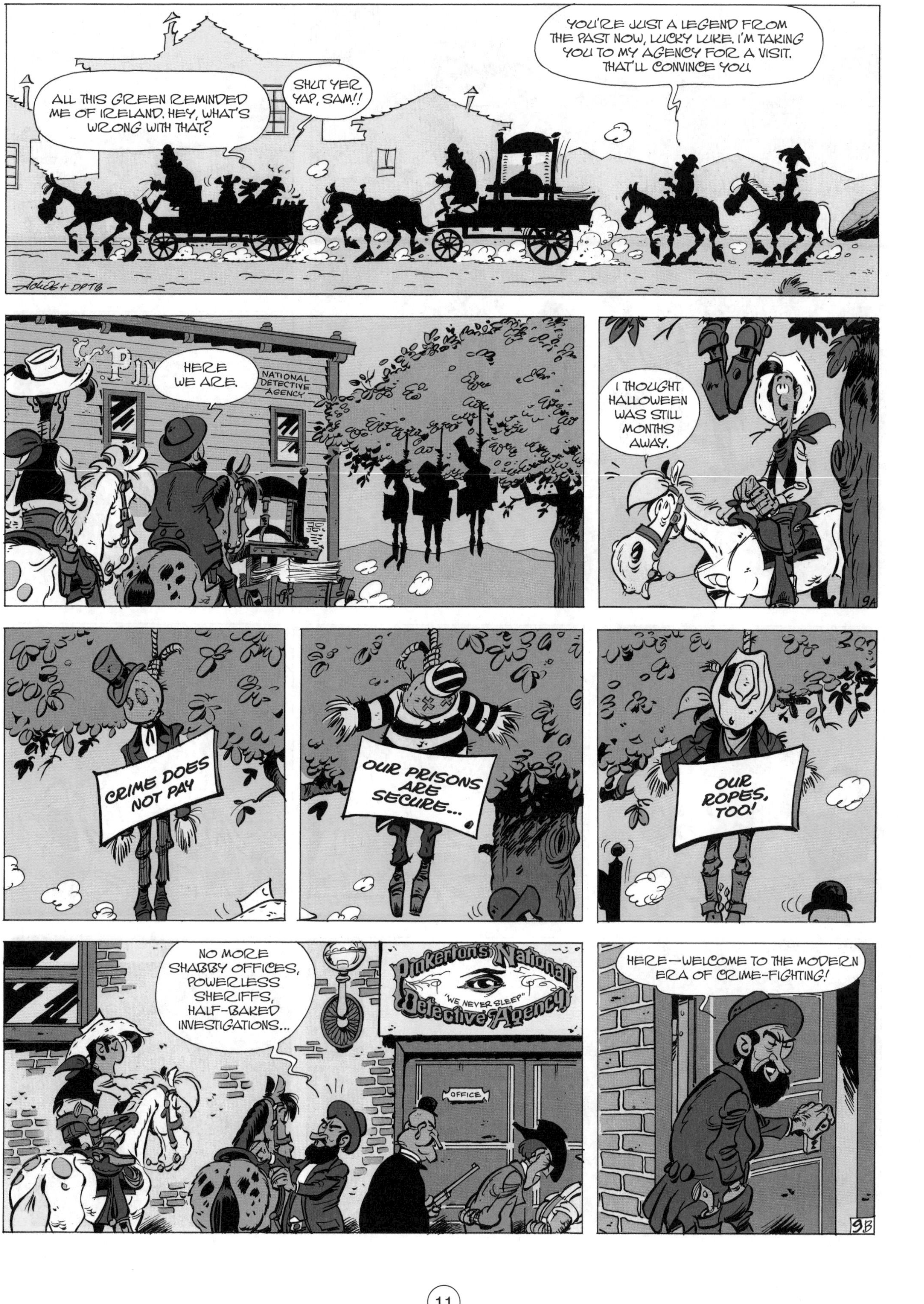
ALL THIS GREEN REMINDED ME OF IRELAND. HEY, WHAT'S WRONG WITH THAT?
SHUT YER YAP, SAM!!
YOU'RE JUST A LEGEND FROM THE PAST NOW, LUCKY LUKE. I'M TAKING YOU TO MY AGENCY FOR A VISIT. THAT'LL CONVINCE YOU.
NATIONAL DETECTIVE AGENCY
HERE WE ARE.
I THOUGHT HALLOWEEN WAS STILL MONTHS AWAY.
CRIME DOES NOT PAY
OUR PRISONS ARE SECURE...
OUR ROPES, TOO!
NO MORE SHABBY OFFICES, POWERLESS SHERIFFS, HALF-BAKED INVESTIGATIONS...
Pinkerton's National Detective Agency
"WE NEVER SLEEP"
OFFICE
HERE—WELCOME TO THE MODERN ERA OF CRIME-FIGHTING!

LOOK...

$ 1000 $ 200

CELLS →
ARCHIVES →

WANTED
$ 1000

WANTED
$ 500

WANTED
ED

WANTED
$ 1000

MR. LUKE, THIS IS THE AGE OF RAPID COMMUNICATION...

ED FLASH ESCAPED 10 MINUTES AGO —STOP—

... CRIMINAL IDENTIFICATION...

STOP SMILING...

07561110 IRON HEAD JOHN

... ANTHROPOMETRICS...

21.5.

21.5.

... SCIENTIFIC INVESTIGATION...

AN INDIAN DELIVERED THE BLOW!

... BY TRUE EXPERTS...

I FOUND RATTLESNAKE VENOM IN HIS WHISKY!

... INTERROGATION...

GROMPH!

WE JUST WANT THE NAMES OF EVERYONE WHO WAS ON THE TRAIN WITH YOU, BILLY.

BUT THERE WERE 15 CARS!

... AND PREVENTATIVE INCARCERATION.

Joe

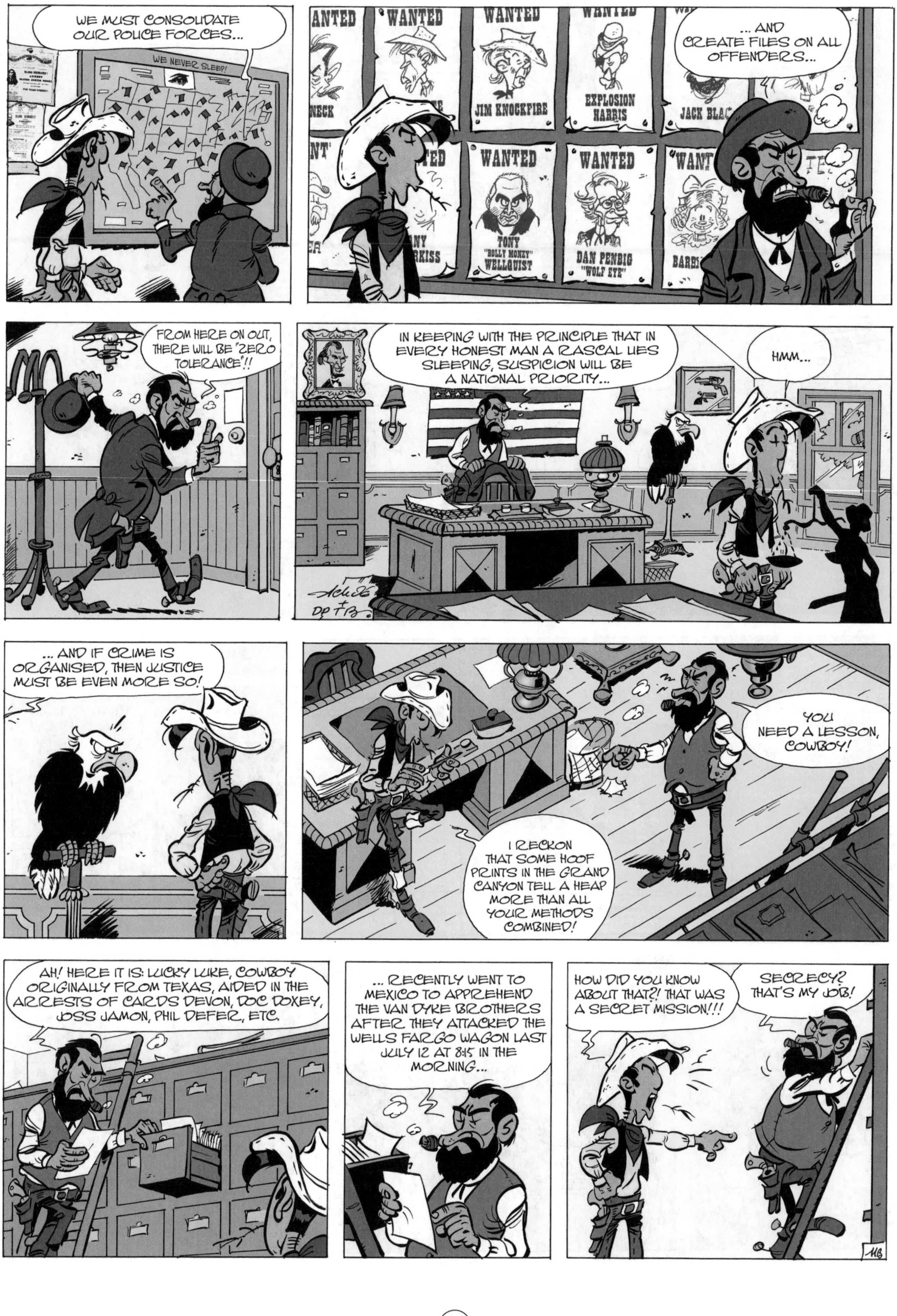
WE MUST CONSOLIDATE OUR POLICE FORCES...
WE NEVER SLEEP!
... AND CREATE FILES ON ALL OFFENDERS...
WANTED
JIM KNOCKFIRE
EXPLOSION HARRIS
TONY "HOLLY MONEY" WELLQUIST
DAN PENBIG "WOLF EYE"
FROM HERE ON OUT, THERE WILL BE "ZERO TOLERANCE"!!
IN KEEPING WITH THE PRINCIPLE THAT IN EVERY HONEST MAN A RASCAL LIES SLEEPING, SUSPICION WILL BE A NATIONAL PRIORITY...
HMM...
... AND IF CRIME IS ORGANISED, THEN JUSTICE MUST BE EVEN MORE SO!
YOU NEED A LESSON, COWBOY!
I RECKON THAT SOME HOOF PRINTS IN THE GRAND CANYON TELL A HEAP MORE THAN ALL YOUR METHODS COMBINED!
AH! HERE IT IS: LUCKY LUKE, COWBOY ORIGINALLY FROM TEXAS, AIDED IN THE ARRESTS OF CARDS DEVON, DOC DOXEY, JOSS JAMON, PHIL DEFER, ETC.
... RECENTLY WENT TO MEXICO TO APPREHEND THE VAN DYKE BROTHERS AFTER THEY ATTACKED THE WELLS FARGO WAGON LAST JULY 12 AT 8:15 IN THE MORNING...
HOW DID YOU KNOW ABOUT THAT?! THAT WAS A SECRET MISSION!!!
SECRECY? THAT'S MY JOB!

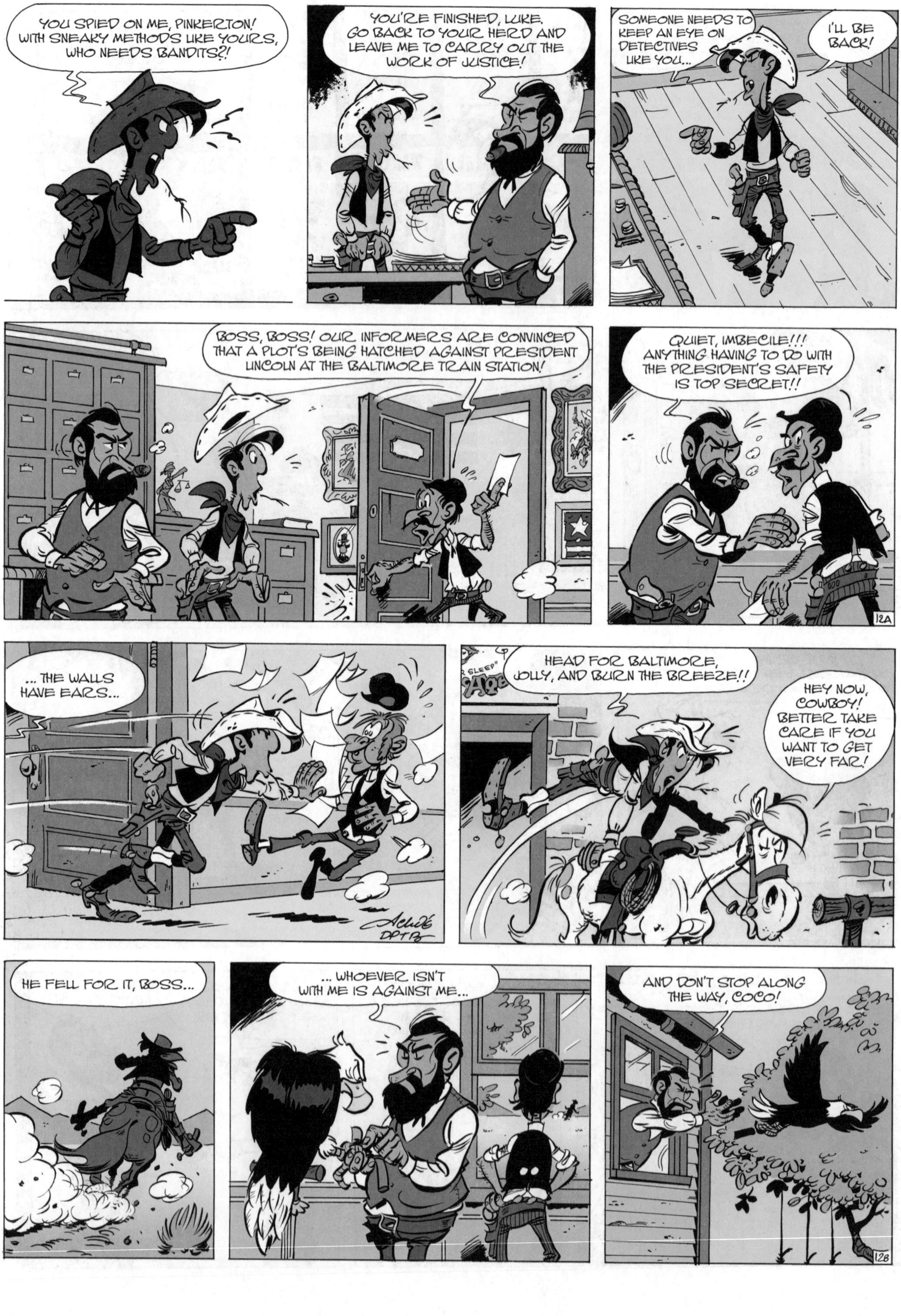
YOU SPIED ON ME, PINKERTON! WITH SNEAKY METHODS LIKE YOURS, WHO NEEDS BANDITS?!
YOU'RE FINISHED, LUKE. GO BACK TO YOUR HERD AND LEAVE ME TO CARRY OUT THE WORK OF JUSTICE!
SOMEONE NEEDS TO KEEP AN EYE ON DETECTIVES LIKE YOU...
I'LL BE BACK!
BOSS, BOSS! OUR INFORMERS ARE CONVINCED THAT A PLOT'S BEING HATCHED AGAINST PRESIDENT LINCOLN AT THE BALTIMORE TRAIN STATION!
QUIET, IMBECILE!!! ANYTHING HAVING TO DO WITH THE PRESIDENT'S SAFETY IS TOP SECRET!!
12A
... THE WALLS HAVE EARS...
HEAD FOR BALTIMORE, JOLLY, AND BURN THE BREEZE!!
HEY NOW, COWBOY! BETTER TAKE CARE IF YOU WANT TO GET VERY FAR!
HE FELL FOR IT, BOSS...
... WHOEVER ISN'T WITH ME IS AGAINST ME...
AND DON'T STOP ALONG THE WAY, COCO!
12B

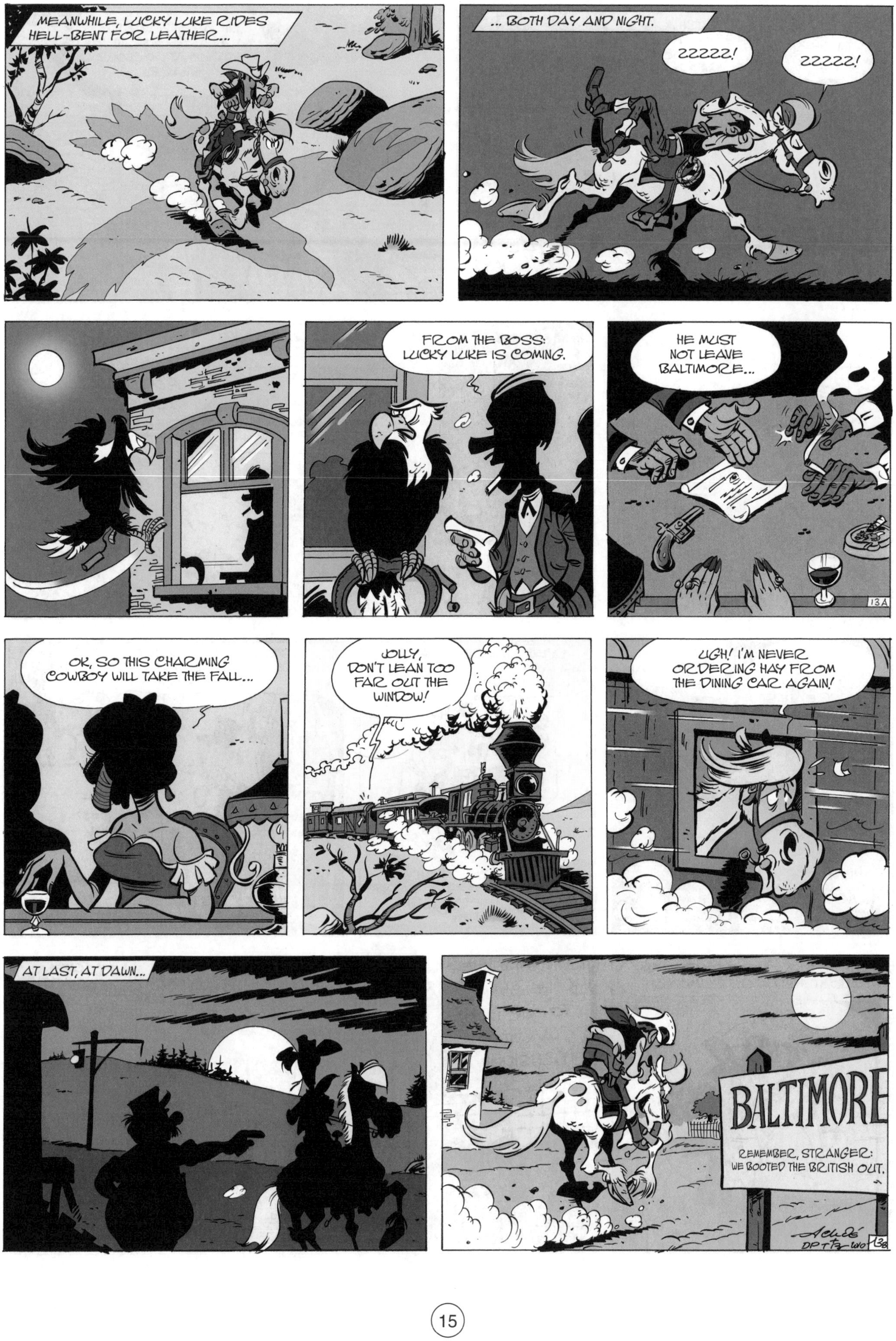
MEANWHILE, LUCKY LUKE RIDES HELL-BENT FOR LEATHER...
... BOTH DAY AND NIGHT.
ZZZZZ!
ZZZZZ!
FROM THE BOSS: LUCKY LUKE IS COMING.
HE MUST NOT LEAVE BALTIMORE...
13A
OK, SO THIS CHARMING COWBOY WILL TAKE THE FALL...
JOLLY, DON'T LEAN TOO FAR OUT THE WINDOW!
UGH! I'M NEVER ORDERING HAY FROM THE DINING CAR AGAIN!
AT LAST, AT DAWN...
BALTIMORE
REMEMBER, STRANGER: WE BOOTED THE BRITISH OUT.
13B

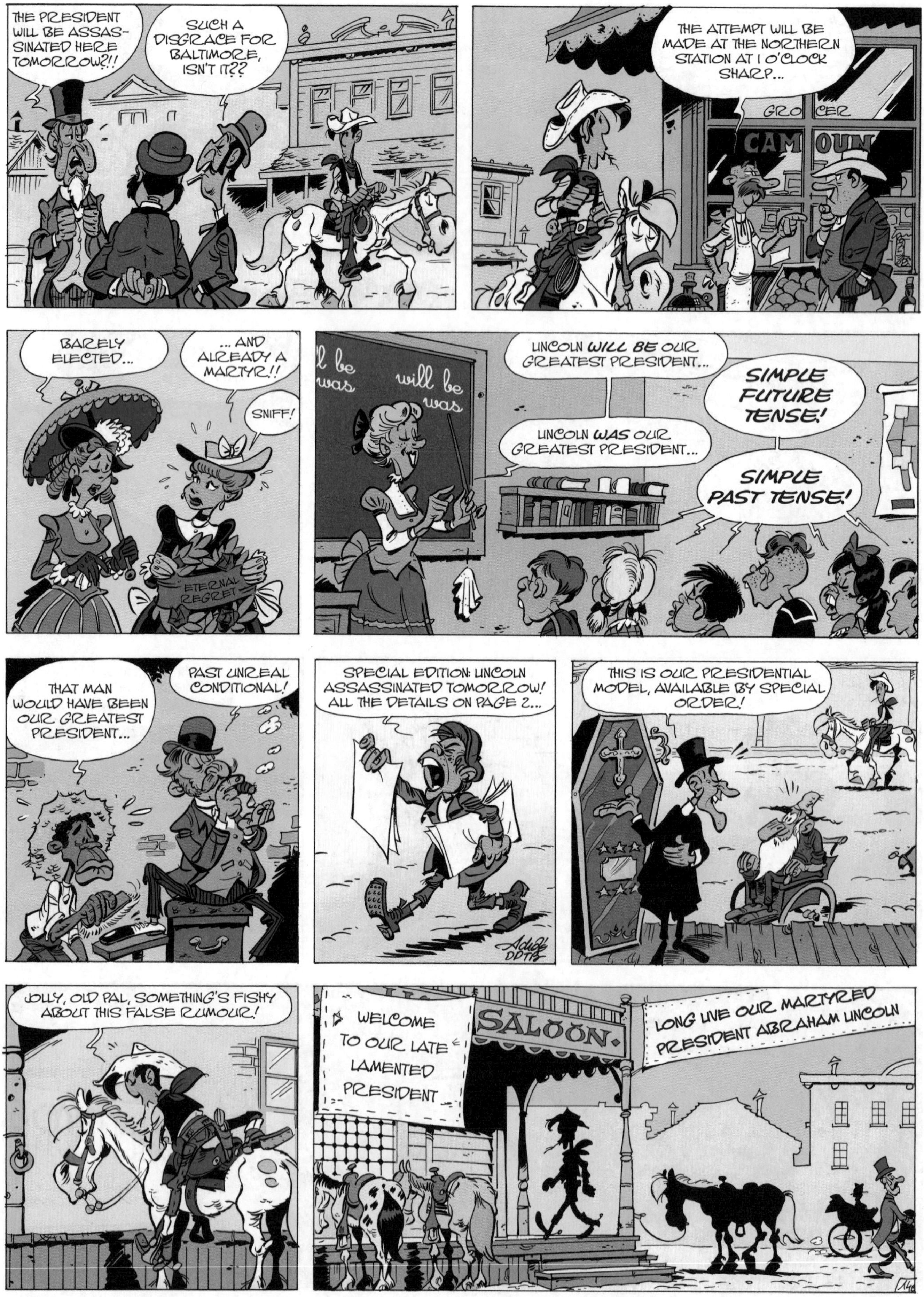
THE PRESIDENT WILL BE ASSASSINATED HERE TOMORROW?!!
SUCH A DISGRACE FOR BALTIMORE, ISN'T IT??
THE ATTEMPT WILL BE MADE AT THE NORTHERN STATION AT 1 O'CLOCK SHARP...
GROCER
CAMOUN
BARELY ELECTED...
... AND ALREADY A MARTYR!!
SNIFF!
ETERNAL REGRET
will be was
LINCOLN WILL BE OUR GREATEST PRESIDENT...
SIMPLE FUTURE TENSE!
LINCOLN WAS OUR GREATEST PRESIDENT...
SIMPLE PAST TENSE!
THAT MAN WOULD HAVE BEEN OUR GREATEST PRESIDENT...
PAST UNREAL CONDITIONAL!
SPECIAL EDITION: LINCOLN ASSASSINATED TOMORROW! ALL THE DETAILS ON PAGE 2...
THIS IS OUR PRESIDENTIAL MODEL, AVAILABLE BY SPECIAL ORDER!
JOLLY, OLD PAL, SOMETHING'S FISHY ABOUT THIS FALSE RUMOUR!
WELCOME TO OUR LATE LAMENTED PRESIDENT
SALOON.
LONG LIVE OUR MARTYRED PRESIDENT ABRAHAM LINCOLN

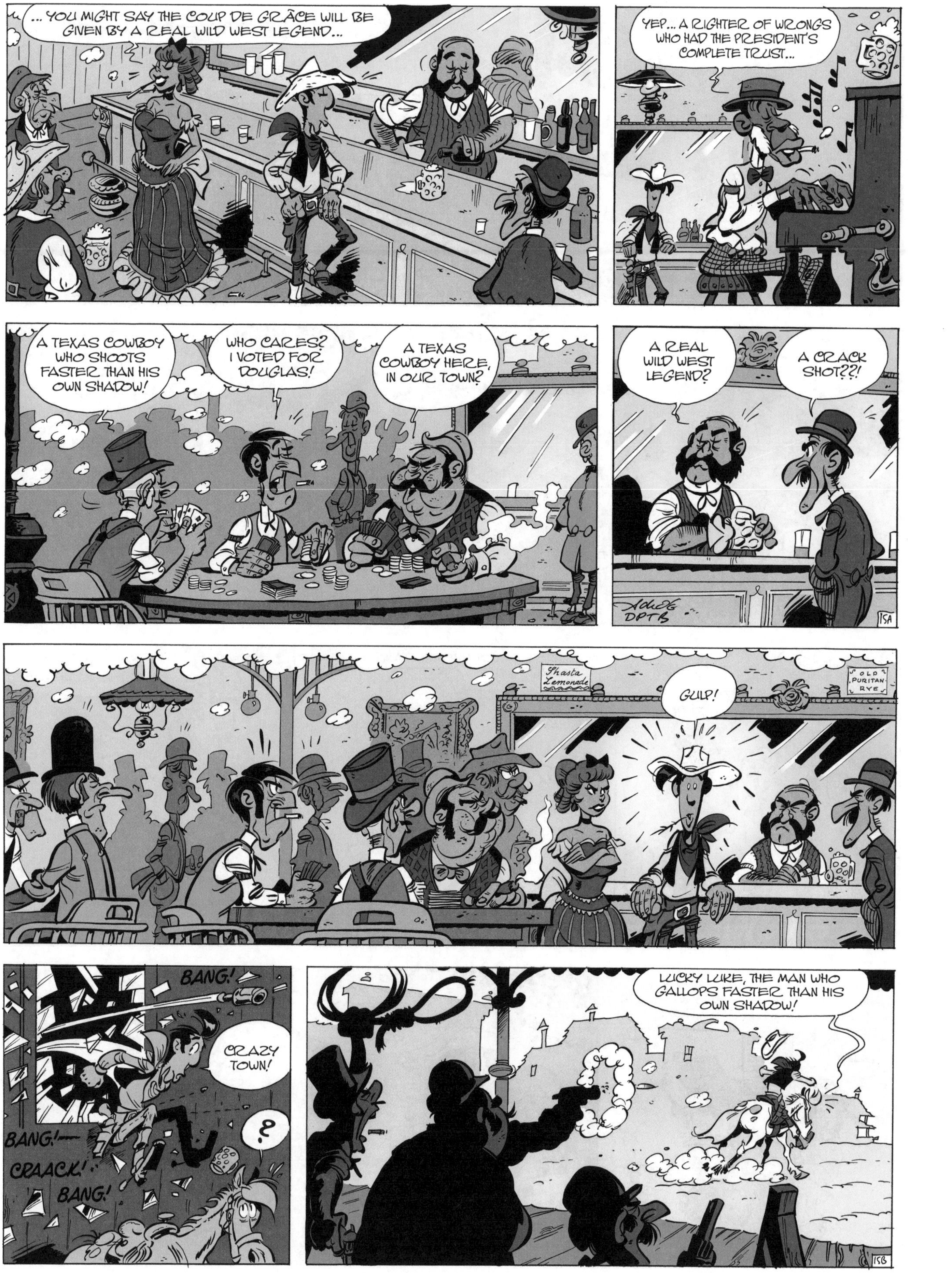
... YOU MIGHT SAY THE COUP DE GRÂCE WILL BE GIVEN BY A REAL WILD WEST LEGEND...
YEP... A RIGHTER OF WRONGS WHO HAD THE PRESIDENT'S COMPLETE TRUST...
A TEXAS COWBOY WHO SHOOTS FASTER THAN HIS OWN SHADOW!
WHO CARES? I VOTED FOR DOUGLAS!
A TEXAS COWBOY HERE, IN OUR TOWN?
A REAL WILD WEST LEGEND?
A CRACK SHOT??!
Shasta Lemonade
OLD PURITAN RYE
GULP!
BANG!
CRAZY TOWN!
BANG!
CRAACK!
BANG!
?
LUCKY LUKE, THE MAN WHO GALLOPS FASTER THAN HIS OWN SHADOW!

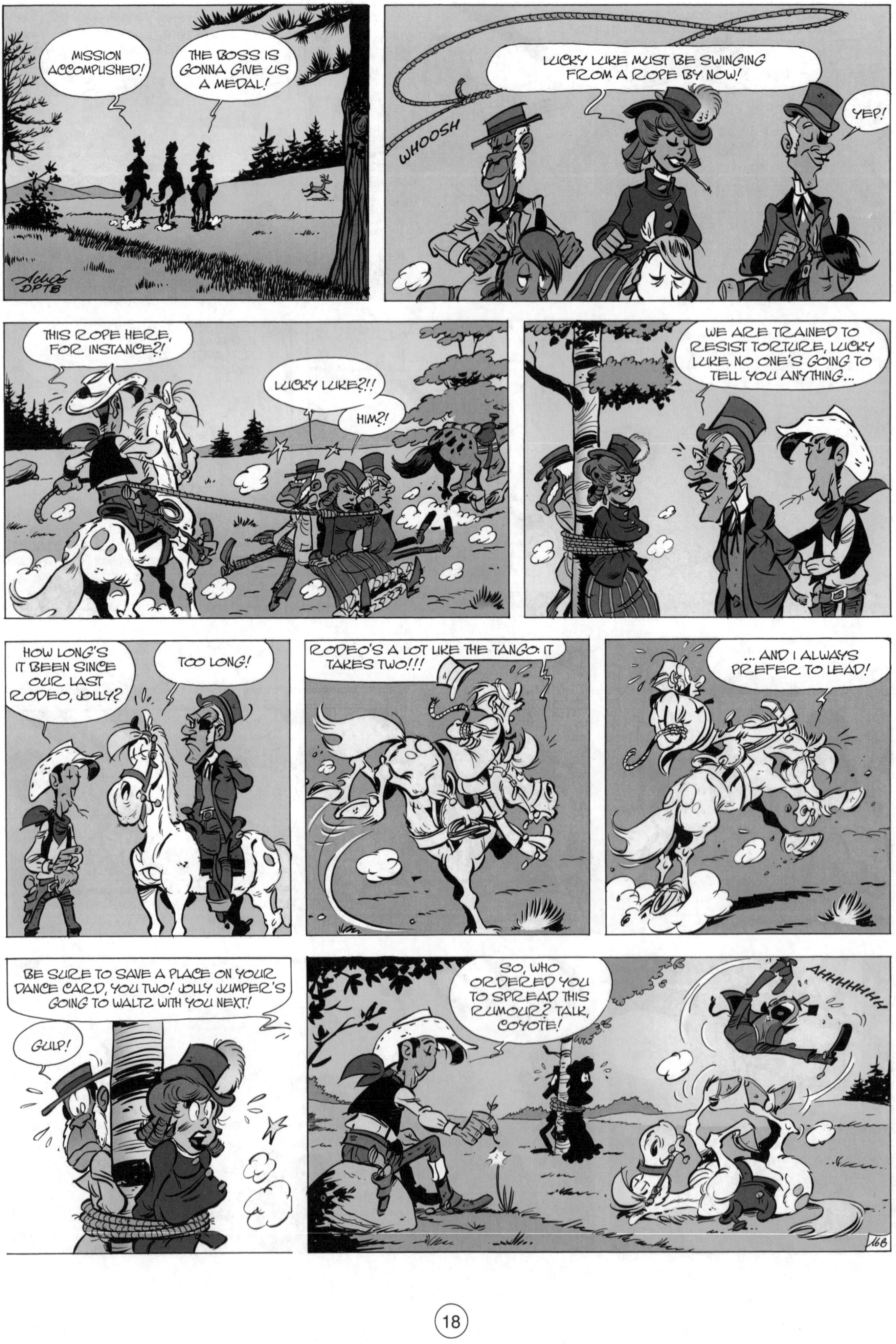

MISSION ACCOMPLISHED!
THE BOSS IS GONNA GIVE US A MEDAL!
LUCKY LUKE MUST BE SWINGING FROM A ROPE BY NOW!
YEP!
WHOOSH
THIS ROPE HERE, FOR INSTANCE?!
LUCKY LUKE?!!
HIM?!
WE ARE TRAINED TO RESIST TORTURE, LUCKY LUKE. NO ONE'S GOING TO TELL YOU ANYTHING...
HOW LONG'S IT BEEN SINCE OUR LAST RODEO, JOLLY?
TOO LONG!
RODEO'S A LOT LIKE THE TANGO: IT TAKES TWO!!!
... AND I ALWAYS PREFER TO LEAD!
BE SURE TO SAVE A PLACE ON YOUR DANCE CARD, YOU TWO! JOLLY JUMPER'S GOING TO WALTZ WITH YOU NEXT!
GULP!
SO, WHO ORDERED YOU TO SPREAD THIS RUMOUR? TALK, COYOTE!
AHHHHHHH

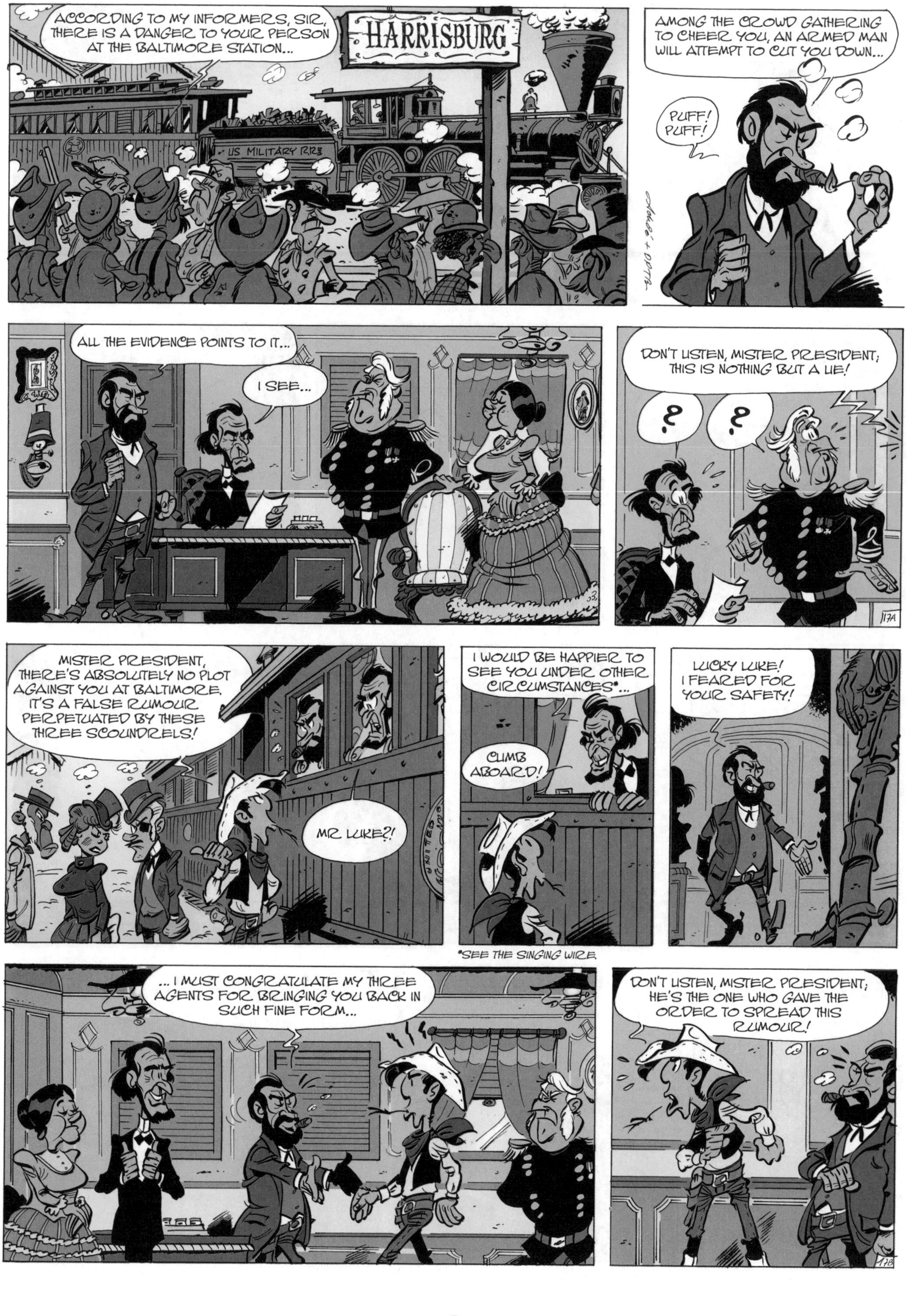
ACCORDING TO MY INFORMERS, SIR, THERE IS A DANGER TO YOUR PERSON AT THE BALTIMORE STATION...
HARRISBURG
AMONG THE CROWD GATHERING TO CHEER YOU, AN ARMED MAN WILL ATTEMPT TO CUT YOU DOWN...
PUFF! PUFF!
ALL THE EVIDENCE POINTS TO IT...
I SEE...
DON'T LISTEN, MISTER PRESIDENT; THIS IS NOTHING BUT A LIE!
?
?
MISTER PRESIDENT, THERE'S ABSOLUTELY NO PLOT AGAINST YOU AT BALTIMORE. IT'S A FALSE RUMOUR PERPETUATED BY THESE THREE SCOUNDRELS!
MR LUKE?!
I WOULD BE HAPPIER TO SEE YOU UNDER OTHER CIRCUMSTANCES*...
CLIMB ABOARD!
LUCKY LUKE! I FEARED FOR YOUR SAFETY!
*SEE THE SINGING WIRE.
... I MUST CONGRATULATE MY THREE AGENTS FOR BRINGING YOU BACK IN SUCH FINE FORM...
DON'T LISTEN, MISTER PRESIDENT; HE'S THE ONE WHO GAVE THE ORDER TO SPREAD THIS RUMOUR!

BUT WHY THE DEVIL WOULD ALLAN DO SUCH A THING?!

WHY? HE'S TRYING TO GAIN YOUR CONFIDENCE IN ORDER TO ENLARGE HIS POWER AND HIS AGENCY. THAT'S WHY!!

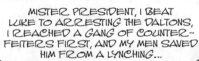

MISTER PRESIDENT, I BEAT LUKE TO ARRESTING THE DALTONS, I REACHED A GANG OF COUNTER-FEITERS FIRST, AND MY MEN SAVED HIM FROM A LYNCHING...

HE'S JEALOUS, AND TRYING TO DISCREDIT ME IN YOUR EYES. THIS ASSASSINATION ATTEMPT IS AUTHENTIC.

WHAT DO YOU THINK, GENERAL BURROUGHS?

YOUR ENEMIES ARE NUMEROUS, AND BALTIMORE IS AN IDEAL PLACE FOR AN ATTACK BY THOSE ✦✱✸☠✦!! SOUTHERNERS!

BEGGING YOUR PAR-DON, SIR!

AND YOU, MY SWEET MARY—WHAT DO YOU THINK?

THAT I DON'T WANT TO WEAR WIDOW'S WEEDS ON THE DAY OF YOUR INAUGURATION, DEAR MR LINCOLN...

SIR, I PLANNED AHEAD: WE WILL GO THROUGH BALTIMORE BY NIGHT AND NO ONE WILL BE THE WISER...

... AND THE AMERICAN PEOPLE WOULDN'T STAND FOR A PRESIDENT IN HIDING!

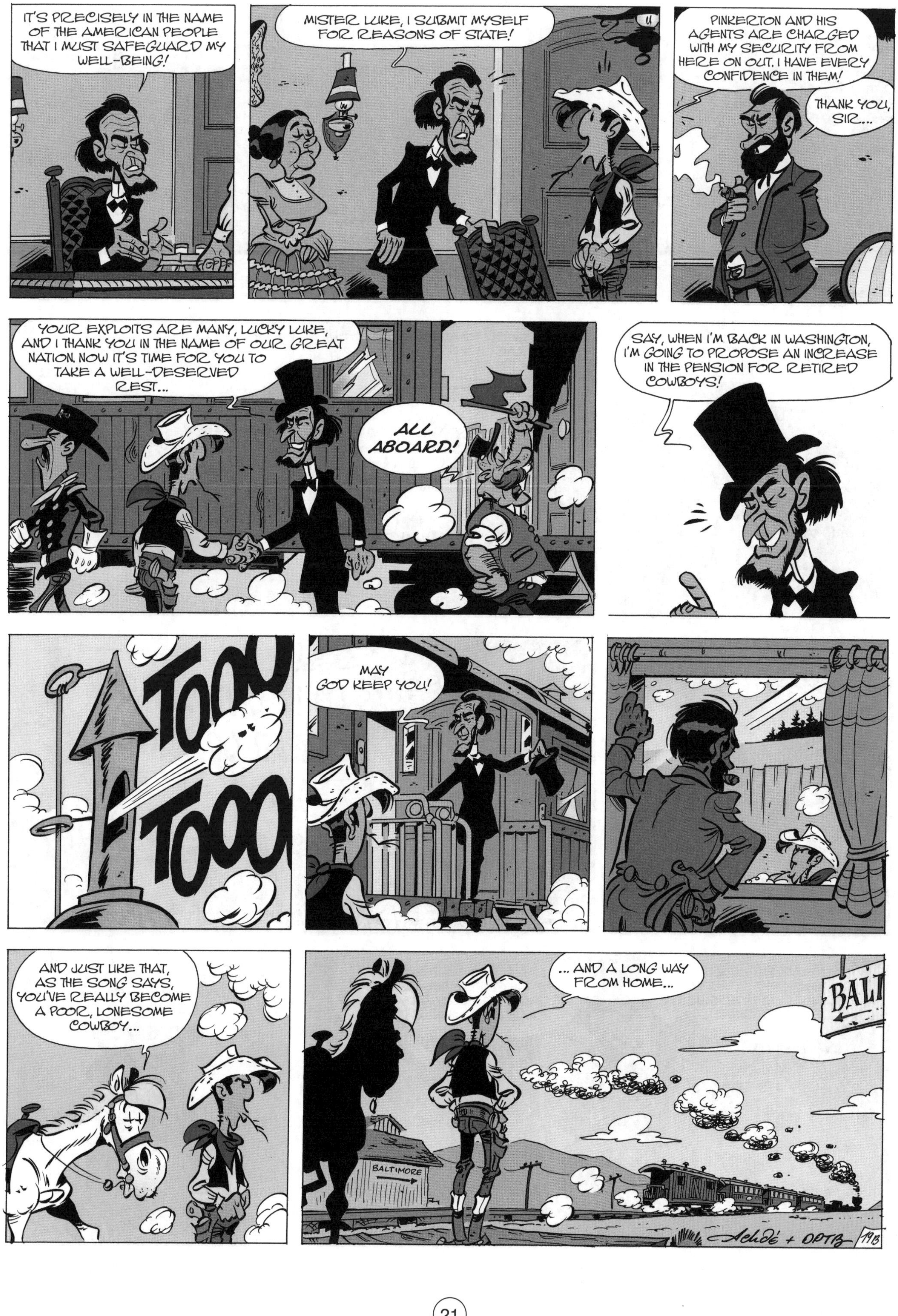
IT'S PRECISELY IN THE NAME OF THE AMERICAN PEOPLE THAT I MUST SAFEGUARD MY WELL-BEING!
MISTER LUKE, I SUBMIT MYSELF FOR REASONS OF STATE!
PINKERTON AND HIS AGENTS ARE CHARGED WITH MY SECURITY FROM HERE ON OUT. I HAVE EVERY CONFIDENCE IN THEM!
THANK YOU, SIR...
YOUR EXPLOITS ARE MANY, LUCKY LUKE, AND I THANK YOU IN THE NAME OF OUR GREAT NATION. NOW IT'S TIME FOR YOU TO TAKE A WELL-DESERVED REST...
ALL ABOARD!
SAY, WHEN I'M BACK IN WASHINGTON, I'M GOING TO PROPOSE AN INCREASE IN THE PENSION FOR RETIRED COWBOYS!
TOOO
TOOO
MAY GOD KEEP YOU!
AND JUST LIKE THAT, AS THE SONG SAYS, YOU'VE REALLY BECOME A POOR, LONESOME COWBOY...
... AND A LONG WAY FROM HOME...
BALTIMORE

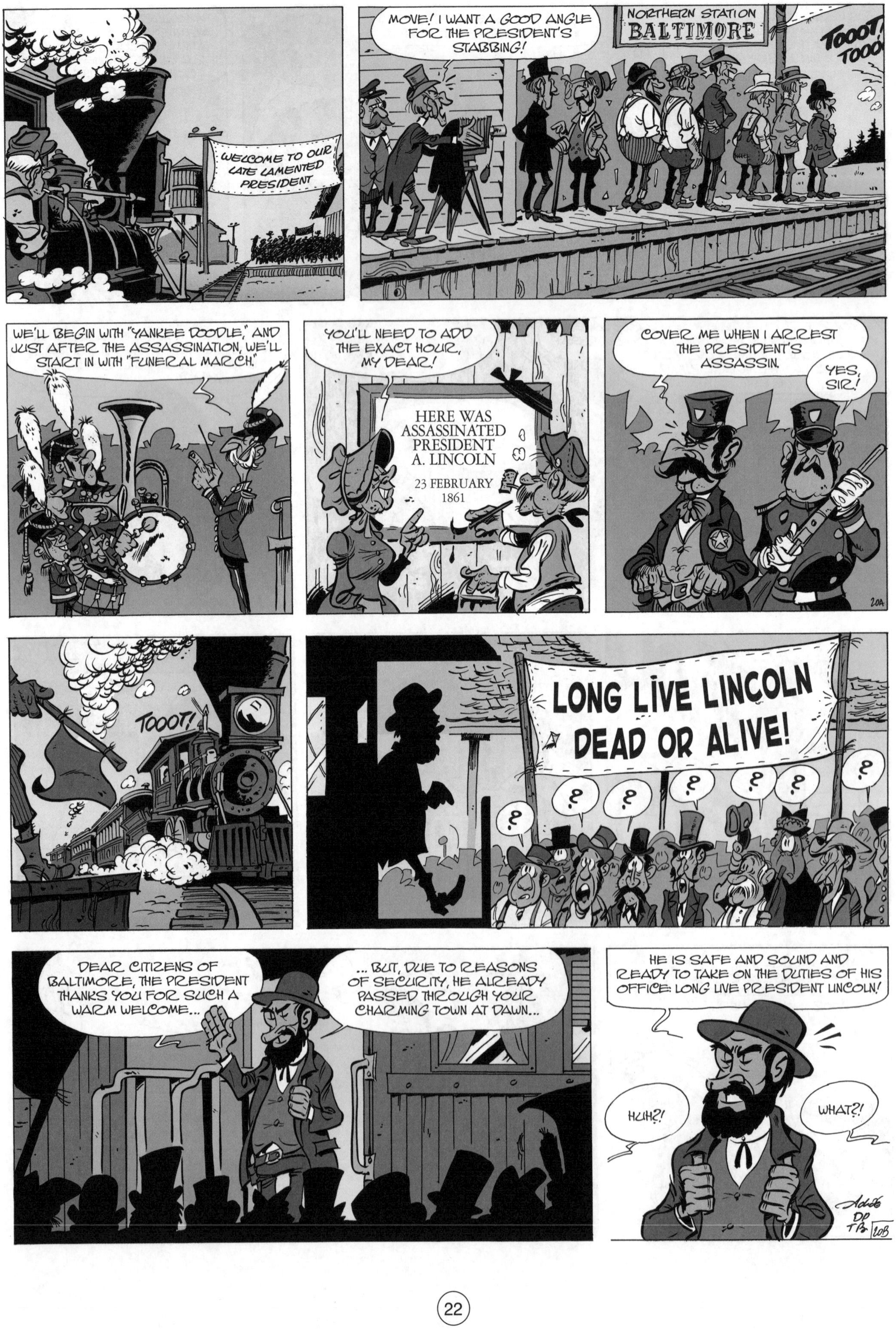
WELCOME TO OUR LATE LAMENTED PRESIDENT
MOVE! I WANT A GOOD ANGLE FOR THE PRESIDENT'S STABBING!
NORTHERN STATION BALTIMORE
TOOOT! TOOO!
WE'LL BEGIN WITH "YANKEE DOODLE," AND JUST AFTER THE ASSASSINATION, WE'LL START IN WITH "FUNERAL MARCH."
YOU'LL NEED TO ADD THE EXACT HOUR, MY DEAR!
HERE WAS ASSASSINATED PRESIDENT A. LINCOLN 23 FEBRUARY 1861
COVER ME WHEN I ARREST THE PRESIDENT'S ASSASSIN.
YES, SIR!
TOOOT!
LONG LIVE LINCOLN DEAD OR ALIVE!
DEAR CITIZENS OF BALTIMORE, THE PRESIDENT THANKS YOU FOR SUCH A WARM WELCOME...
... BUT, DUE TO REASONS OF SECURITY, HE ALREADY PASSED THROUGH YOUR CHARMING TOWN AT DAWN...
HE IS SAFE AND SOUND AND READY TO TAKE ON THE DUTIES OF HIS OFFICE: LONG LIVE PRESIDENT LINCOLN!
HUH?!
WHAT?!

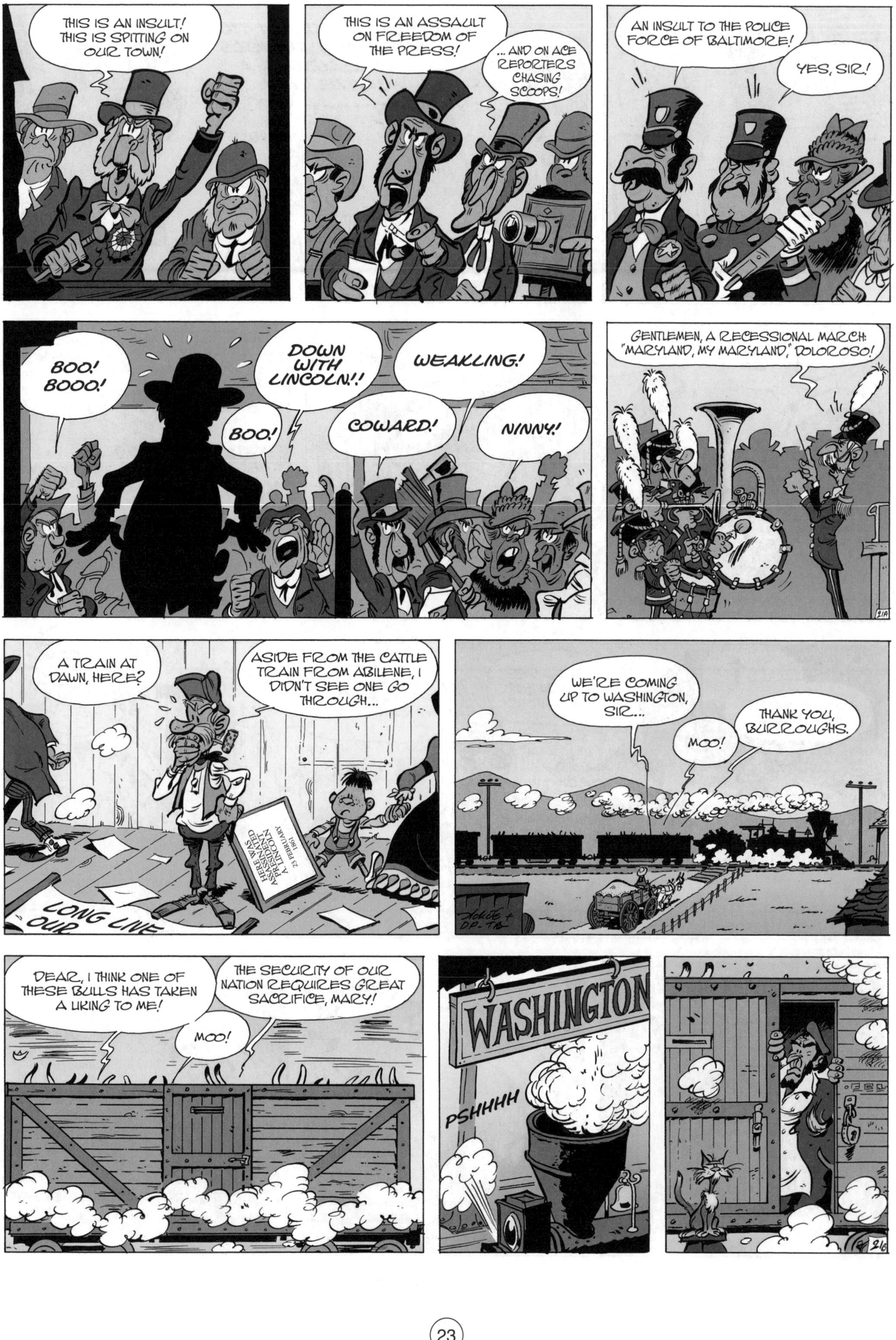
THIS IS AN INSULT! THIS IS SPITTING ON OUR TOWN!
THIS IS AN ASSAULT ON FREEDOM OF THE PRESS!
... AND ON ACE REPORTERS CHASING SCOOPS!
AN INSULT TO THE POLICE FORCE OF BALTIMORE!
YES, SIR!
BOO! BOOO!
DOWN WITH LINCOLN!!
WEAKLING!
BOO!
COWARD!
NINNY!
GENTLEMEN, A RECESSIONAL MARCH: "MARYLAND, MY MARYLAND," DOLOROSO!
A TRAIN AT DAWN, HERE?
ASIDE FROM THE CATTLE TRAIN FROM ABILENE, I DIDN'T SEE ONE GO THROUGH...
HERE WAS ASSASSINATED PRESIDENT A. LINCOLN 23 FEBRUARY 1861
LONG LIVE OUR
WE'RE COMING UP TO WASHINGTON, SIR...
MOO!
THANK YOU, BURROUGHS.
DEAR, I THINK ONE OF THESE BULLS HAS TAKEN A LIKING TO ME!
THE SECURITY OF OUR NATION REQUIRES GREAT SACRIFICE, MARY!
MOO!
WASHINGTON
PSHHHH

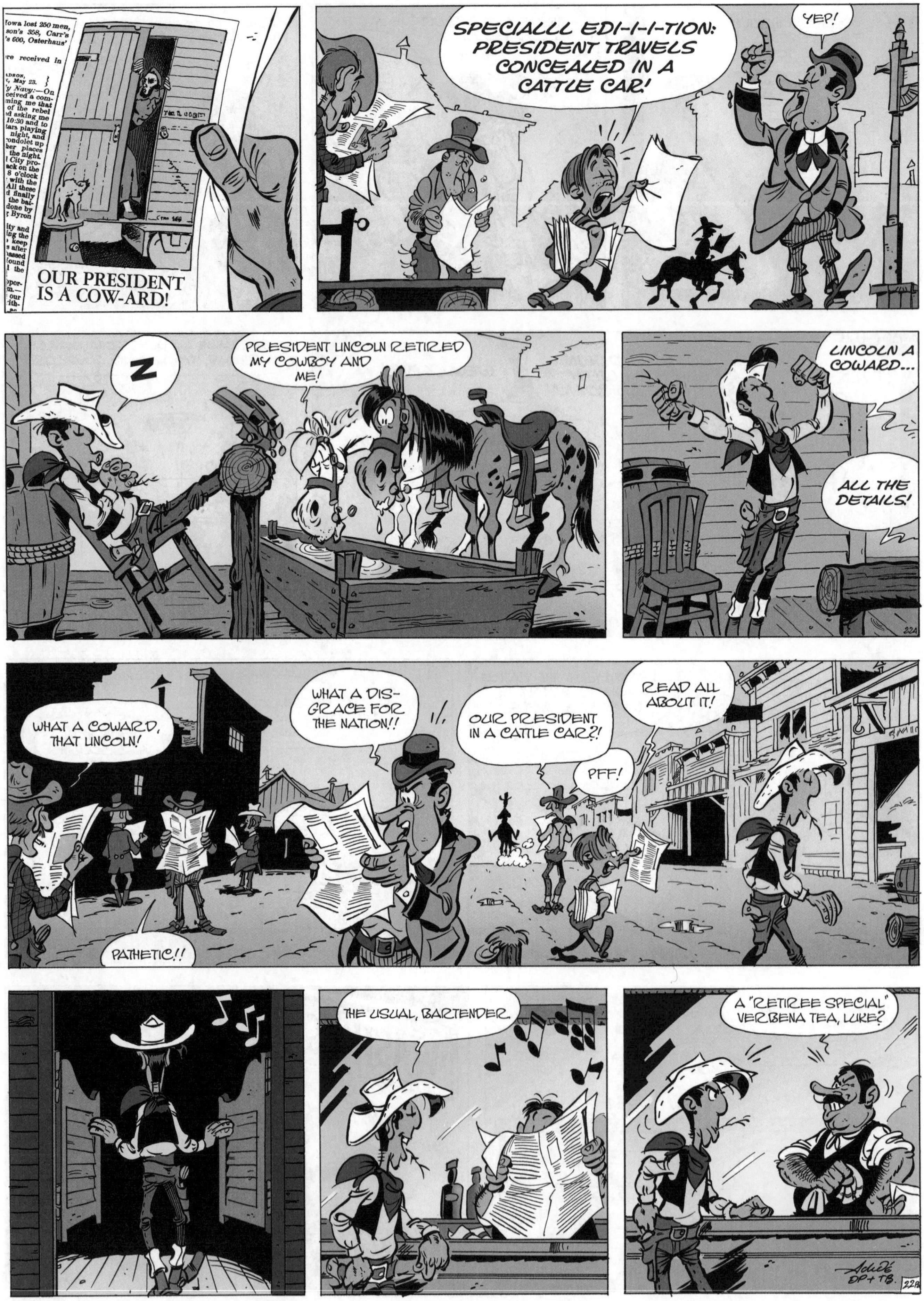
OUR PRESIDENT IS A COW-ARD!
SPECIALLL EDI-I-I-TION: PRESIDENT TRAVELS CONCEALED IN A CATTLE CAR!
YEP!
Z
PRESIDENT LINCOLN RETIRED MY COWBOY AND ME!
LINCOLN A COWARD...
ALL THE DETAILS!
WHAT A COWARD, THAT LINCOLN!
WHAT A DIS-GRACE FOR THE NATION!!
OUR PRESIDENT IN A CATTLE CAR?!
READ ALL ABOUT IT!
PFF!
PATHETIC!!
THE USUAL, BARTENDER.
A "RETIREE SPECIAL" VERBENA TEA, LUKE?

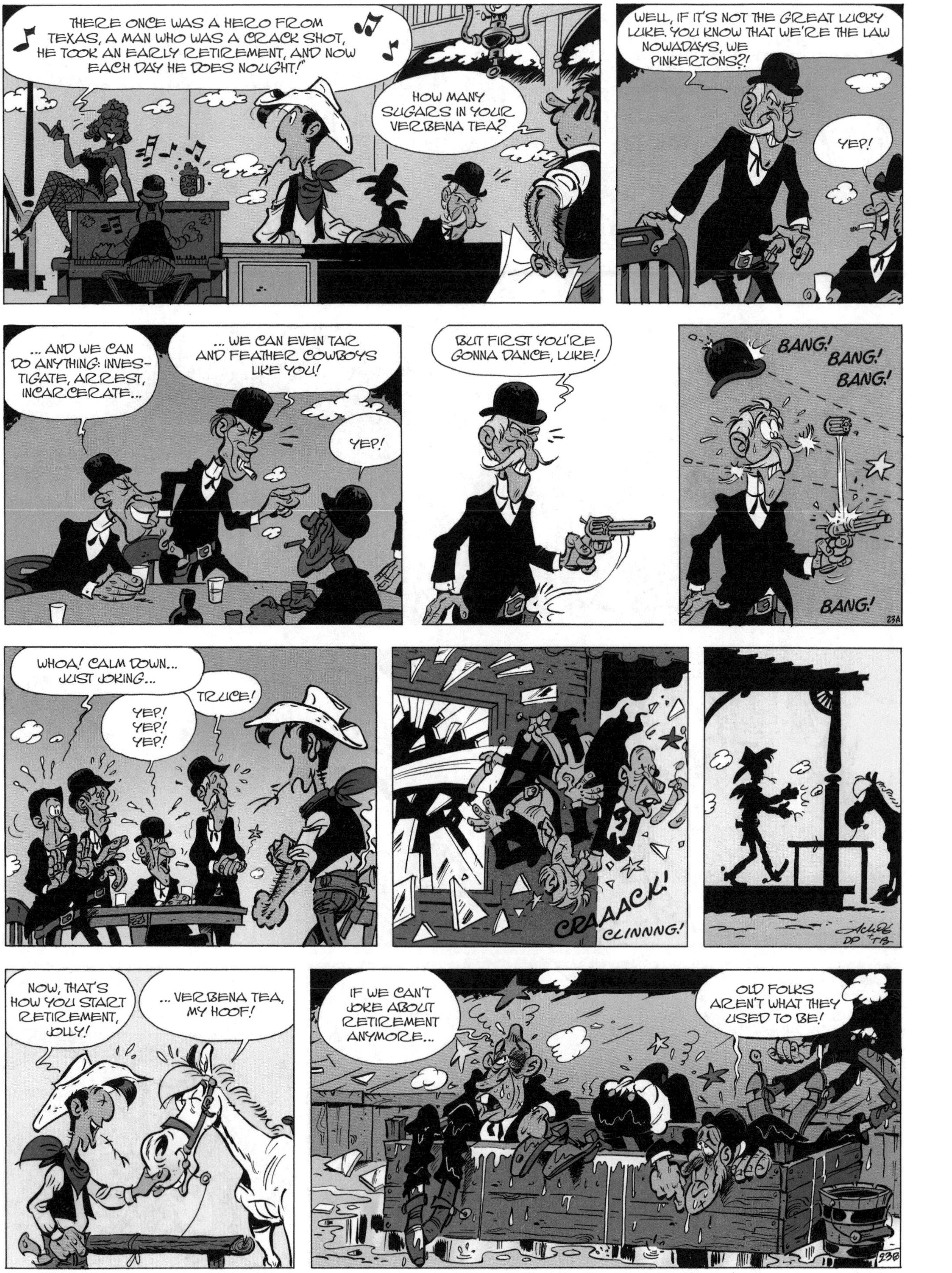
THERE ONCE WAS A HERO FROM TEXAS, A MAN WHO WAS A CRACK SHOT, HE TOOK AN EARLY RETIREMENT, AND NOW EACH DAY HE DOES NOUGHT!"
HOW MANY SUGARS IN YOUR VERBENA TEA?
WELL, IF IT'S NOT THE GREAT LUCKY LUKE. YOU KNOW THAT WE'RE THE LAW NOWADAYS, WE PINKERTONS?!
YEP!
... AND WE CAN DO ANYTHING: INVESTIGATE, ARREST, INCARCERATE...
... WE CAN EVEN TAR AND FEATHER COWBOYS LIKE YOU!
YEP!
BUT FIRST YOU'RE GONNA DANCE, LUKE!
BANG!
BANG!
BANG!
BANG!
23A
WHOA! CALM DOWN... JUST JOKING...
YEP! YEP! YEP!
TRUCE!
CRAAACK!
CLINNNG!
NOW, THAT'S HOW YOU START RETIREMENT, JOLLY!
... VERBENA TEA, MY HOOF!
IF WE CAN'T JOKE ABOUT RETIREMENT ANYMORE...
OLD FOLKS AREN'T WHAT THEY USED TO BE!
23B

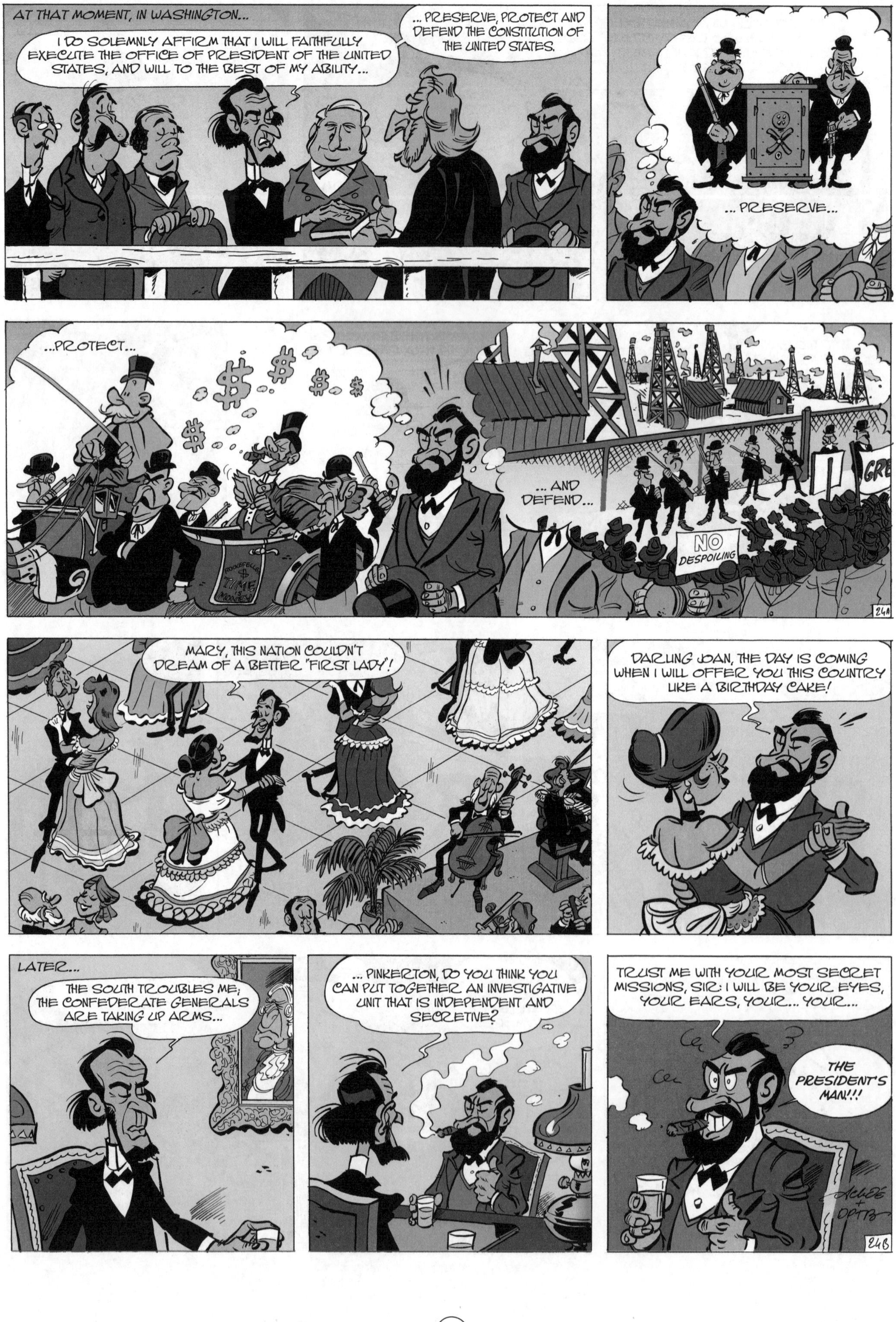
AT THAT MOMENT, IN WASHINGTON...
I DO SOLEMNLY AFFIRM THAT I WILL FAITHFULLY EXECUTE THE OFFICE OF PRESIDENT OF THE UNITED STATES, AND WILL TO THE BEST OF MY ABILITY...
... PRESERVE, PROTECT AND DEFEND THE CONSTITUTION OF THE UNITED STATES.
... PRESERVE...
...PROTECT...
... AND DEFEND...
NO DESPOILING
MARY, THIS NATION COULDN'T DREAM OF A BETTER "FIRST LADY"!
DARLING JOAN, THE DAY IS COMING WHEN I WILL OFFER YOU THIS COUNTRY LIKE A BIRTHDAY CAKE!
LATER...
THE SOUTH TROUBLES ME; THE CONFEDERATE GENERALS ARE TAKING UP ARMS...
... PINKERTON, DO YOU THINK YOU CAN PUT TOGETHER AN INVESTIGATIVE UNIT THAT IS INDEPENDENT AND SECRETIVE?
TRUST ME WITH YOUR MOST SECRET MISSIONS, SIR: I WILL BE YOUR EYES, YOUR EARS, YOUR... YOUR...
THE PRESIDENT'S MAN!!!

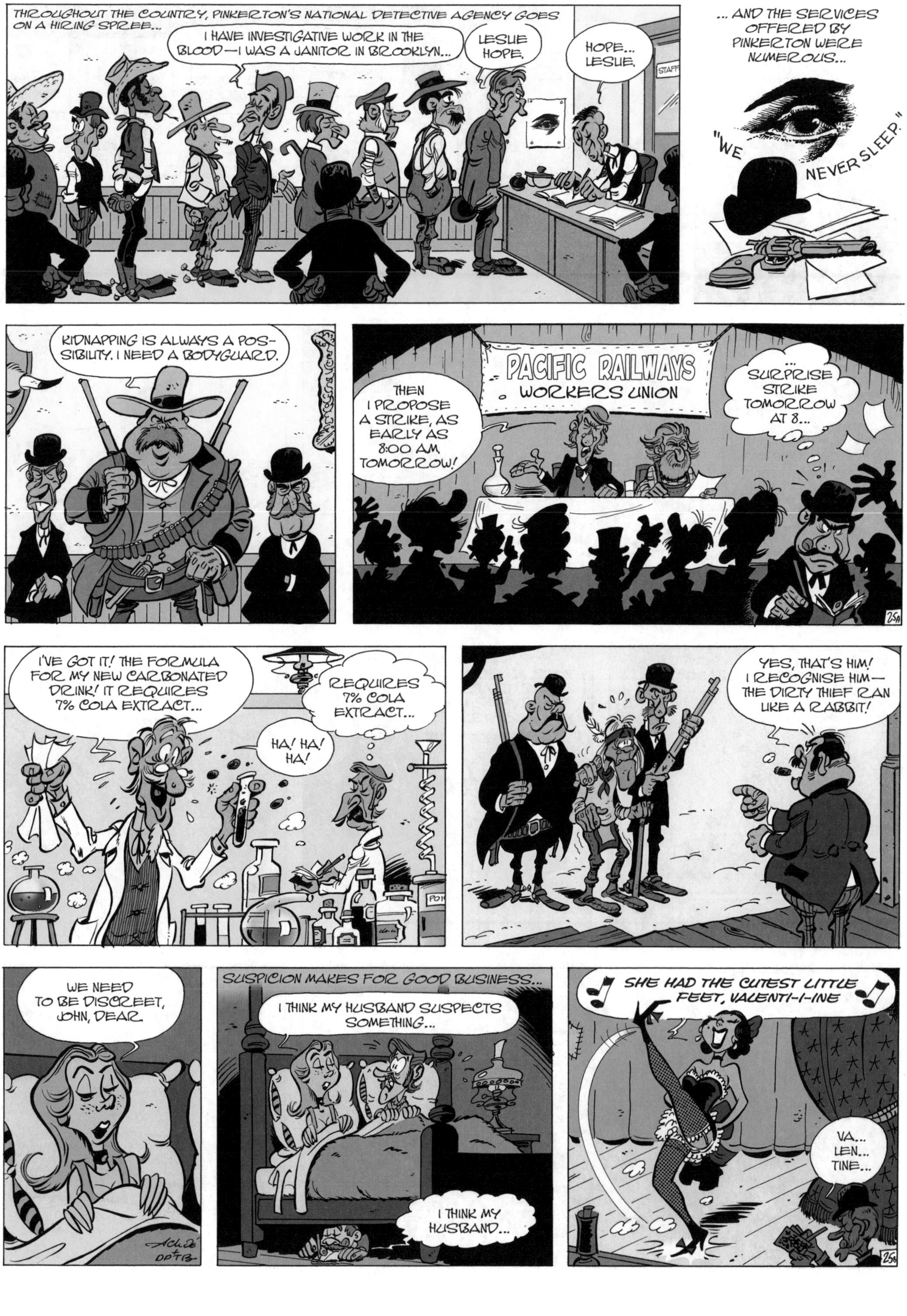
THROUGHOUT THE COUNTRY, PINKERTON'S NATIONAL DETECTIVE AGENCY GOES ON A HIRING SPREE...
I HAVE INVESTIGATIVE WORK IN THE BLOOD—I WAS A JANITOR IN BROOKLYN...
LESLIE HOPE.
HOPE... LESLIE.
STAFF
... AND THE SERVICES OFFERED BY PINKERTON WERE NUMEROUS...
"WE NEVER SLEEP."
KIDNAPPING IS ALWAYS A POSSIBILITY. I NEED A BODYGUARD.
PACIFIC RAILWAYS
WORKERS UNION
THEN I PROPOSE A STRIKE, AS EARLY AS 8:00 AM TOMORROW!
... SURPRISE STRIKE TOMORROW AT 8...
I'VE GOT IT! THE FORMULA FOR MY NEW CARBONATED DRINK! IT REQUIRES 7% COLA EXTRACT...
REQUIRES 7% COLA EXTRACT...
HA! HA! HA!
YES, THAT'S HIM! I RECOGNISE HIM—THE DIRTY THIEF RAN LIKE A RABBIT!
WE NEED TO BE DISCREET, JOHN, DEAR.
SUSPICION MAKES FOR GOOD BUSINESS...
I THINK MY HUSBAND SUSPECTS SOMETHING...
I THINK MY HUSBAND...
SHE HAD THE CUTEST LITTLE FEET, VALENTI-I-INE
VA... LEN... TINE...

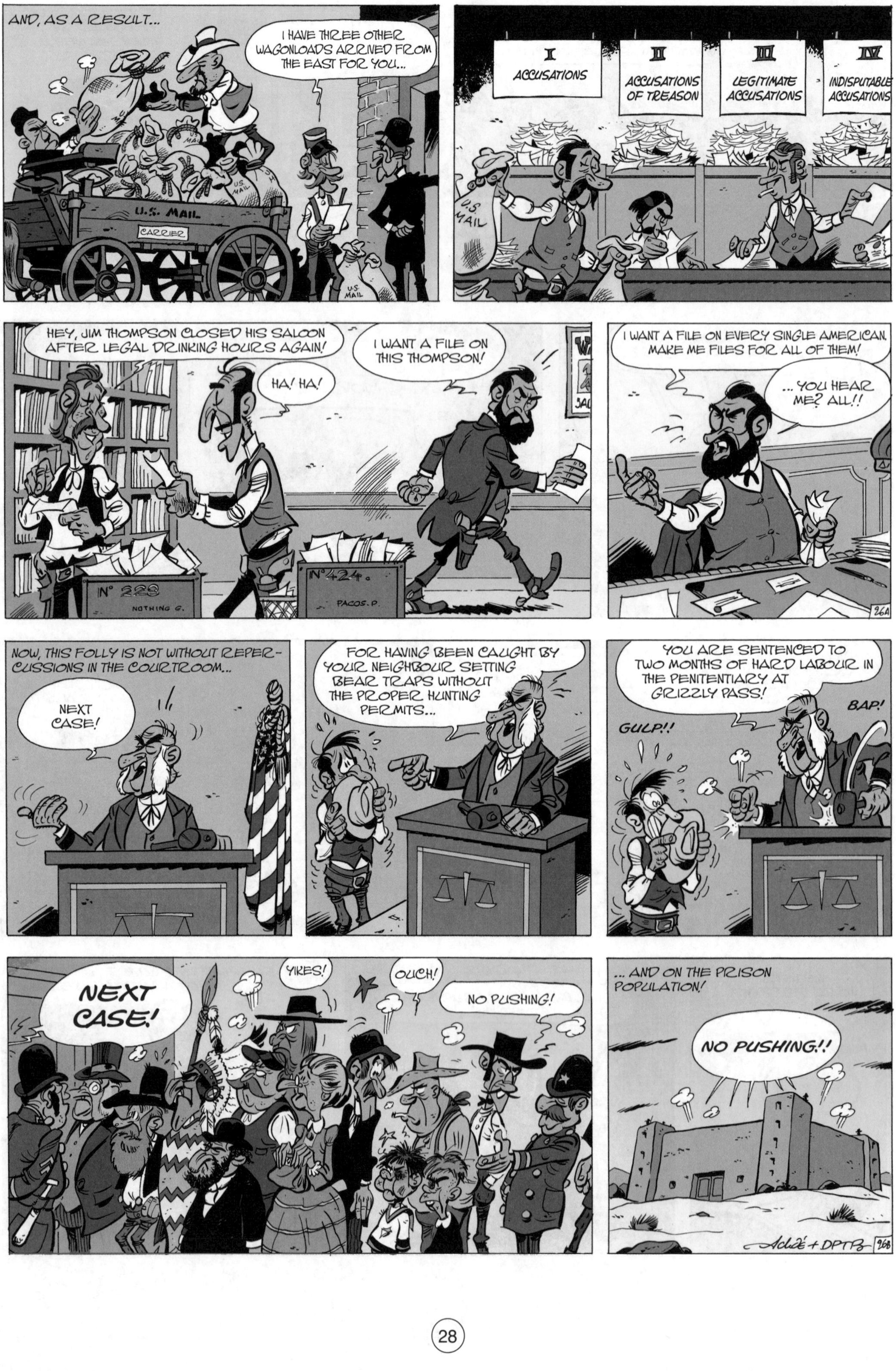
AND, AS A RESULT...
I HAVE THREE OTHER WAGONLOADS ARRIVED FROM THE EAST FOR YOU...
U.S. MAIL
CARRIER
I ACCUSATIONS
II ACCUSATIONS OF TREASON
III LEGITIMATE ACCUSATIONS
IV INDISPUTABLE ACCUSATIONS
HEY, JIM THOMPSON CLOSED HIS SALOON AFTER LEGAL DRINKING HOURS AGAIN!
HA! HA!
I WANT A FILE ON THIS THOMPSON!
N° 229 NOTHING G.
N° 424 PACOS. P.
I WANT A FILE ON EVERY SINGLE AMERICAN. MAKE ME FILES FOR ALL OF THEM!
...YOU HEAR ME? ALL!!
NOW, THIS FOLLY IS NOT WITHOUT REPERCUSSIONS IN THE COURTROOM...
NEXT CASE!
FOR HAVING BEEN CAUGHT BY YOUR NEIGHBOUR SETTING BEAR TRAPS WITHOUT THE PROPER HUNTING PERMITS...
YOU ARE SENTENCED TO TWO MONTHS OF HARD LABOUR IN THE PENITENTIARY AT GRIZZLY PASS!
GULP!!
BAP!
NEXT CASE!
YIKES!
OUCH!
NO PUSHING!
... AND ON THE PRISON POPULATION!
NO PUSHING!!

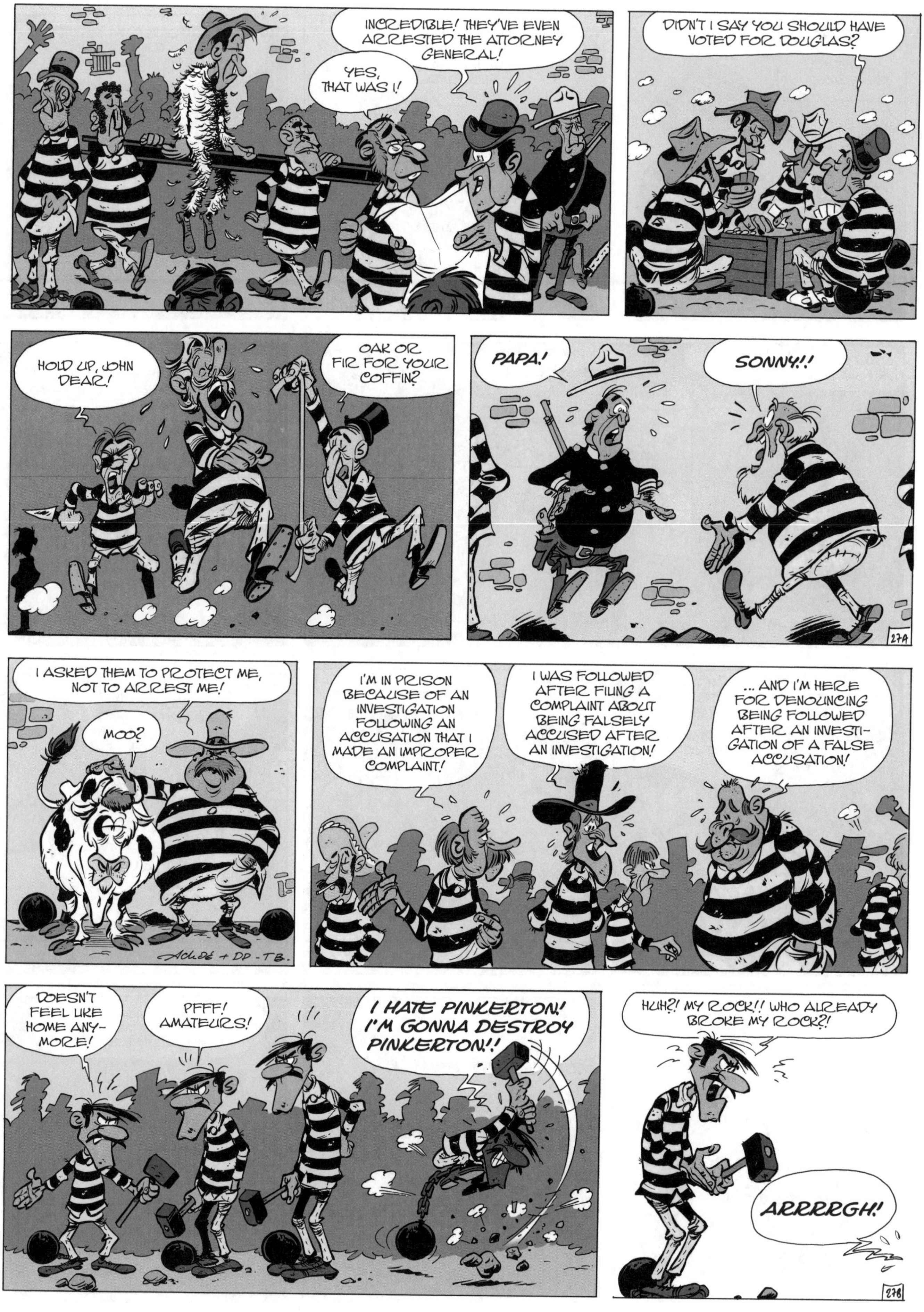
INCREDIBLE! THEY'VE EVEN ARRESTED THE ATTORNEY GENERAL!
YES, THAT WAS I!
DIDN'T I SAY YOU SHOULD HAVE VOTED FOR DOUGLAS?
HOLD UP, JOHN DEAR!
OAK OR FIR FOR YOUR COFFIN?
PAPA!
SONNY!!
27A
I ASKED THEM TO PROTECT ME, NOT TO ARREST ME!
MOO?
Achdé + DP - TB.
I'M IN PRISON BECAUSE OF AN INVESTIGATION FOLLOWING AN ACCUSATION THAT I MADE AN IMPROPER COMPLAINT!
I WAS FOLLOWED AFTER FILING A COMPLAINT ABOUT BEING FALSELY ACCUSED AFTER AN INVESTIGATION!
... AND I'M HERE FOR DENOUNCING BEING FOLLOWED AFTER AN INVESTIGATION OF A FALSE ACCUSATION!
DOESN'T FEEL LIKE HOME ANYMORE!
PFFF! AMATEURS!
I HATE PINKERTON! I'M GONNA DESTROY PINKERTON!!
HUH?! MY ROCK!! WHO ALREADY BROKE MY ROCK?!
ARRRRGH!
27B

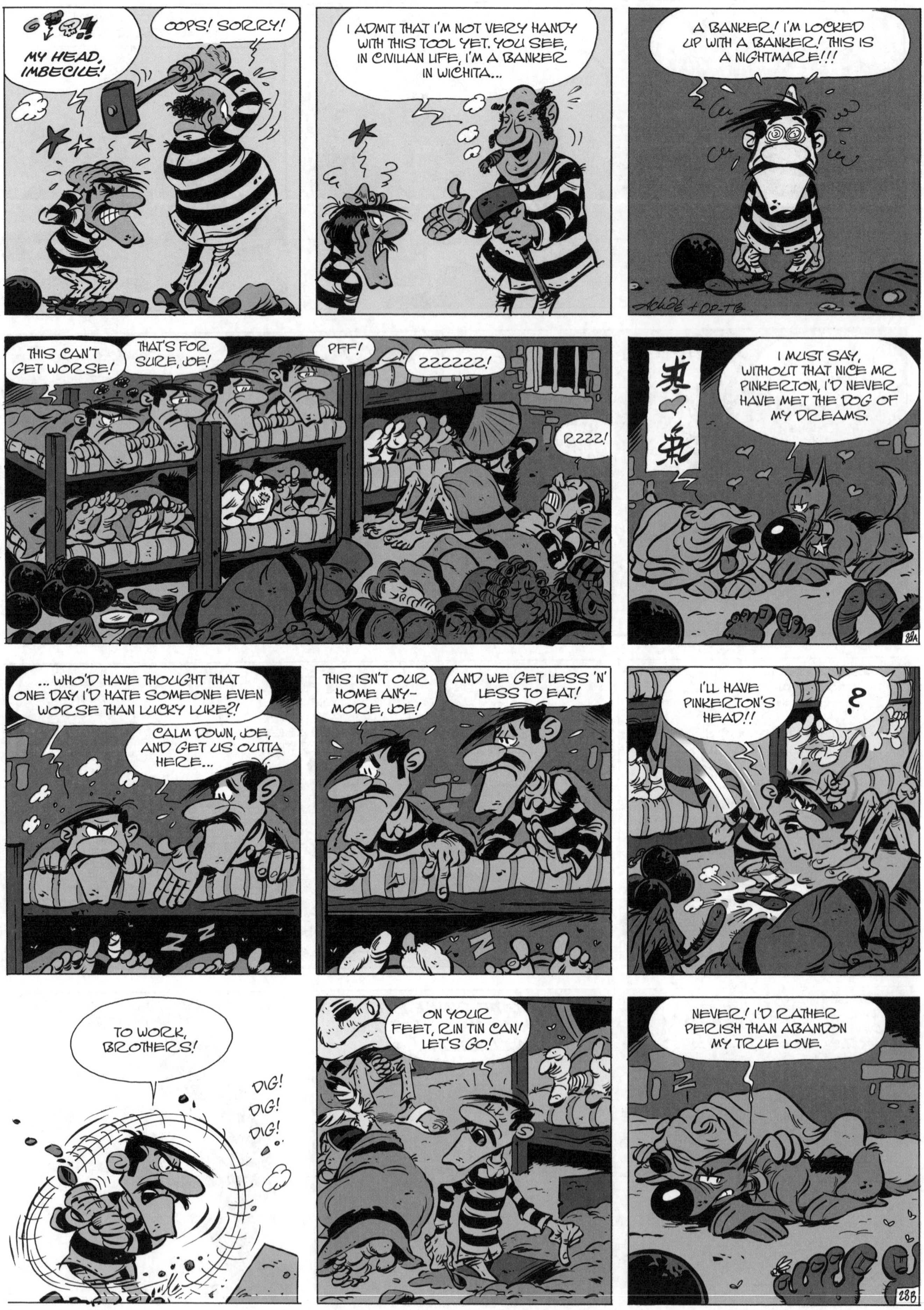
MY HEAD, IMBECILE!
OOPS! SORRY!
I ADMIT THAT I'M NOT VERY HANDY WITH THIS TOOL YET. YOU SEE, IN CIVILIAN LIFE, I'M A BANKER IN WICHITA...
A BANKER! I'M LOCKED UP WITH A BANKER! THIS IS A NIGHTMARE!!!
THIS CAN'T GET WORSE!
THAT'S FOR SURE, JOE!
PFF!
ZZZZZZ!
RZZZ!
I MUST SAY, WITHOUT THAT NICE MR PINKERTON, I'D NEVER HAVE MET THE DOG OF MY DREAMS.
... WHO'D HAVE THOUGHT THAT ONE DAY I'D HATE SOMEONE EVEN WORSE THAN LUCKY LUKE?!
CALM DOWN, JOE, AND GET US OUTTA HERE...
Z Z
THIS ISN'T OUR HOME ANY-MORE, JOE!
AND WE GET LESS 'N' LESS TO EAT!
Z
I'LL HAVE PINKERTON'S HEAD!!
?
TO WORK, BROTHERS!
DIG! DIG! DIG!
ON YOUR FEET, RIN TIN CAN! LET'S GO!
NEVER! I'D RATHER PERISH THAN ABANDON MY TRUE LOVE.

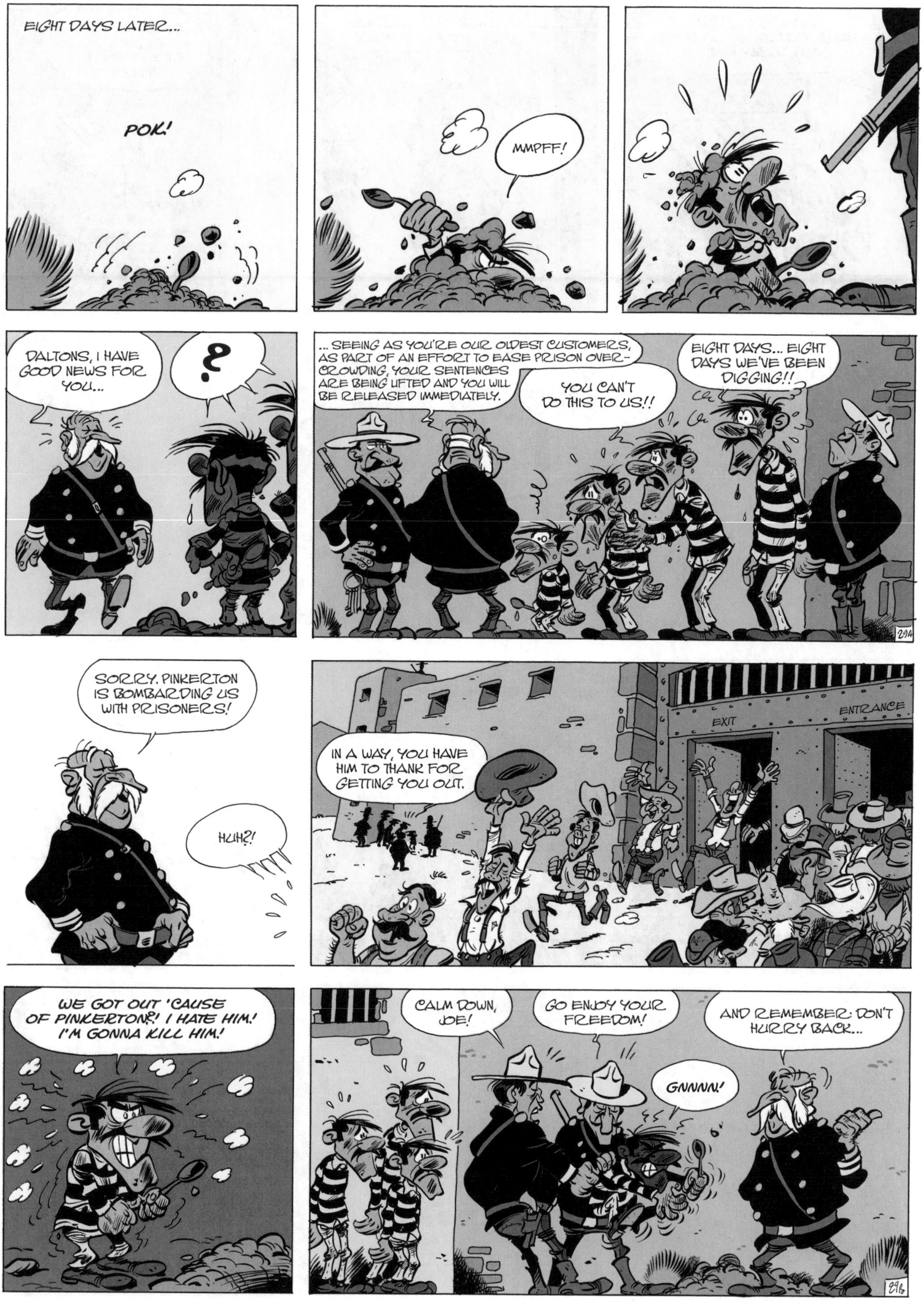

EIGHT DAYS LATER...
POK!
MMPFF!
DALTONS, I HAVE GOOD NEWS FOR YOU...
?
... SEEING AS YOU'RE OUR OLDEST CUSTOMERS, AS PART OF AN EFFORT TO EASE PRISON OVER-CROWDING, YOUR SENTENCES ARE BEING LIFTED AND YOU WILL BE RELEASED IMMEDIATELY.
YOU CAN'T DO THIS TO US!!
EIGHT DAYS... EIGHT DAYS WE'VE BEEN DIGGING!!
SORRY. PINKERTON IS BOMBARDING US WITH PRISONERS!
HUH?!
IN A WAY, YOU HAVE HIM TO THANK FOR GETTING YOU OUT.
EXIT
ENTRANCE
WE GOT OUT 'CAUSE OF PINKERTON?! I HATE HIM! I'M GONNA KILL HIM!
CALM DOWN, JOE!
GO ENJOY YOUR FREEDOM!
GNNNN!
AND REMEMBER: DON'T HURRY BACK...

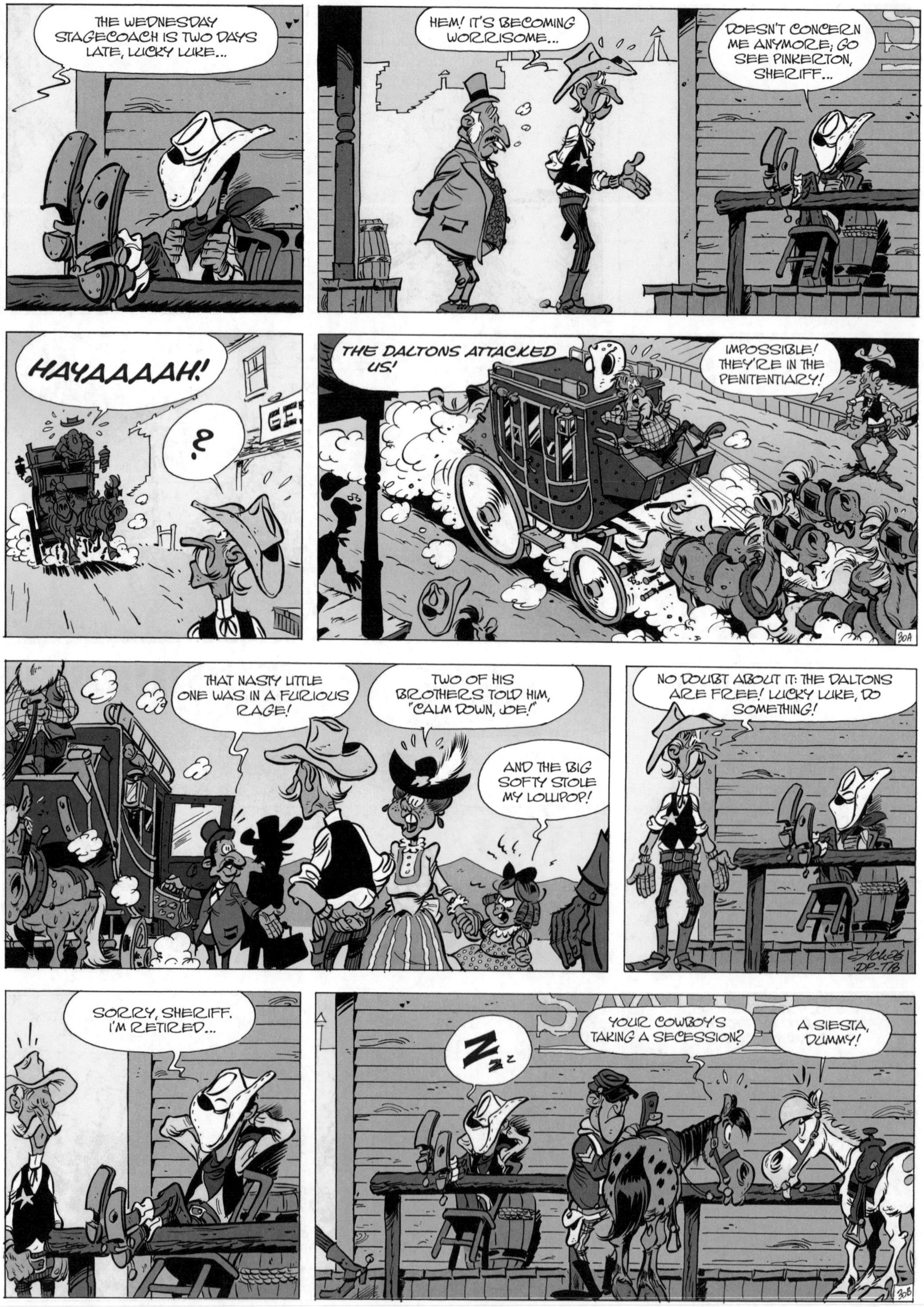
THE WEDNESDAY STAGECOACH IS TWO DAYS LATE, LUCKY LUKE...
HEM! IT'S BECOMING WORRISOME...
DOESN'T CONCERN ME ANYMORE; GO SEE PINKERTON, SHERIFF...
HAYAAAAAH!
?
THE DALTONS ATTACKED US!
IMPOSSIBLE! THEY'RE IN THE PENITENTIARY!
30A
THAT NASTY LITTLE ONE WAS IN A FURIOUS RAGE!
TWO OF HIS BROTHERS TOLD HIM, "CALM DOWN, JOE!"
AND THE BIG SOFTY STOLE MY LOLLIPOP!
NO DOUBT ABOUT IT: THE DALTONS ARE FREE! LUCKY LUKE, DO SOMETHING!
SORRY, SHERIFF. I'M RETIRED...
Z
YOUR COWBOY'S TAKING A SECESSION?
A SIESTA, DUMMY!
30B

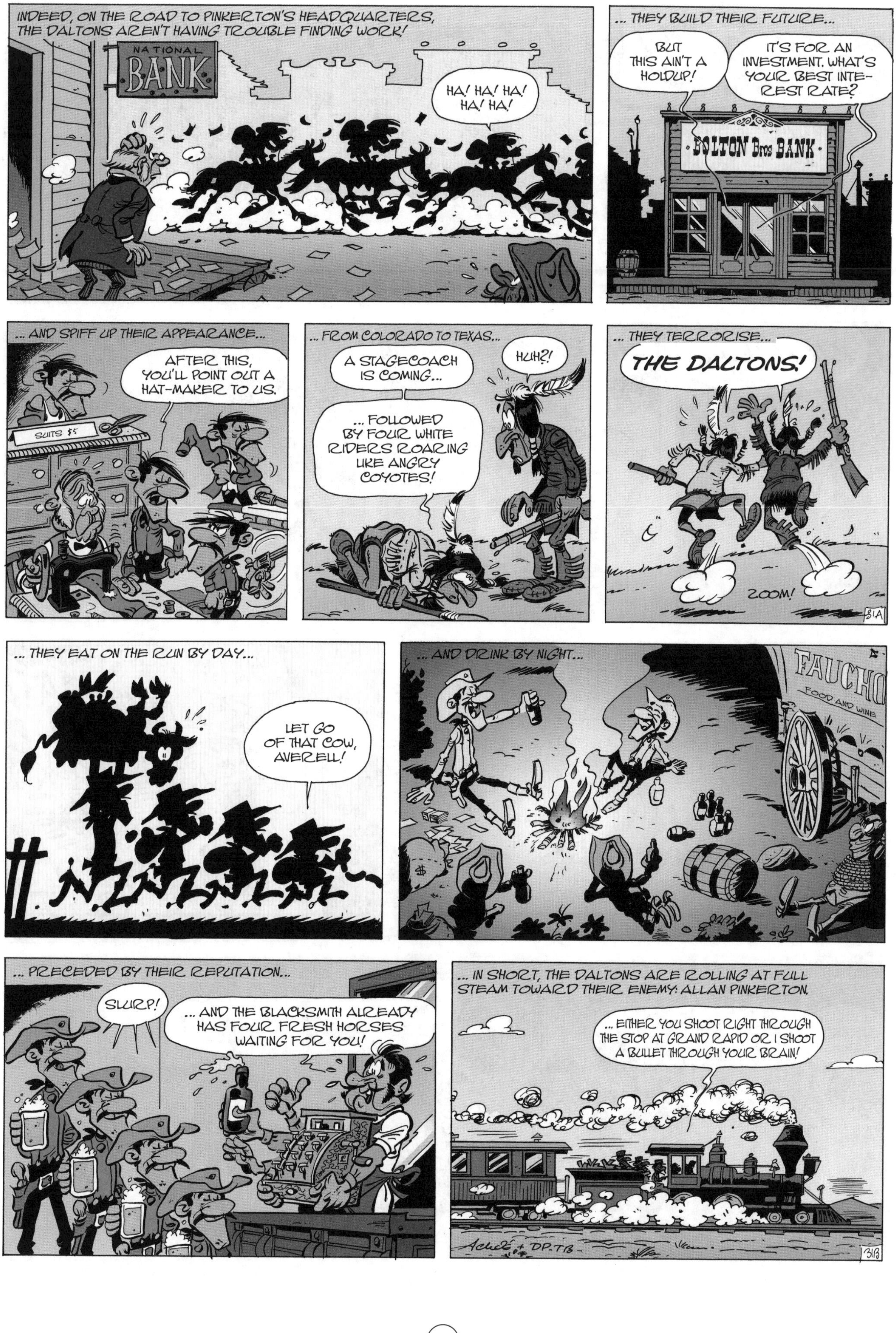
INDEED, ON THE ROAD TO PINKERTON'S HEADQUARTERS, THE DALTONS AREN'T HAVING TROUBLE FINDING WORK!
NATIONAL BANK
HA! HA! HA! HA! HA!
... THEY BUILD THEIR FUTURE...
BUT THIS AIN'T A HOLDUP!
IT'S FOR AN INVESTMENT. WHAT'S YOUR BEST INTEREST RATE?
BOLTON Bros BANK
... AND SPIFF UP THEIR APPEARANCE...
AFTER THIS, YOU'LL POINT OUT A HAT-MAKER TO US.
SUITS $5
... FROM COLORADO TO TEXAS...
A STAGECOACH IS COMING...
... FOLLOWED BY FOUR WHITE RIDERS ROARING LIKE ANGRY COYOTES!
HUH?!
... THEY TERRORISE...
THE DALTONS!
ZOOM!
... THEY EAT ON THE RUN BY DAY...
LET GO OF THAT COW, AVERELL!
... AND DRINK BY NIGHT...
FAUCHO
FOOD AND WINE
... PRECEDED BY THEIR REPUTATION...
SLURP!
... AND THE BLACKSMITH ALREADY HAS FOUR FRESH HORSES WAITING FOR YOU!
... IN SHORT, THE DALTONS ARE ROLLING AT FULL STEAM TOWARD THEIR ENEMY: ALLAN PINKERTON.
... EITHER YOU SHOOT RIGHT THROUGH THE STOP AT GRAND RAPID OR I SHOOT A BULLET THROUGH YOUR BRAIN!

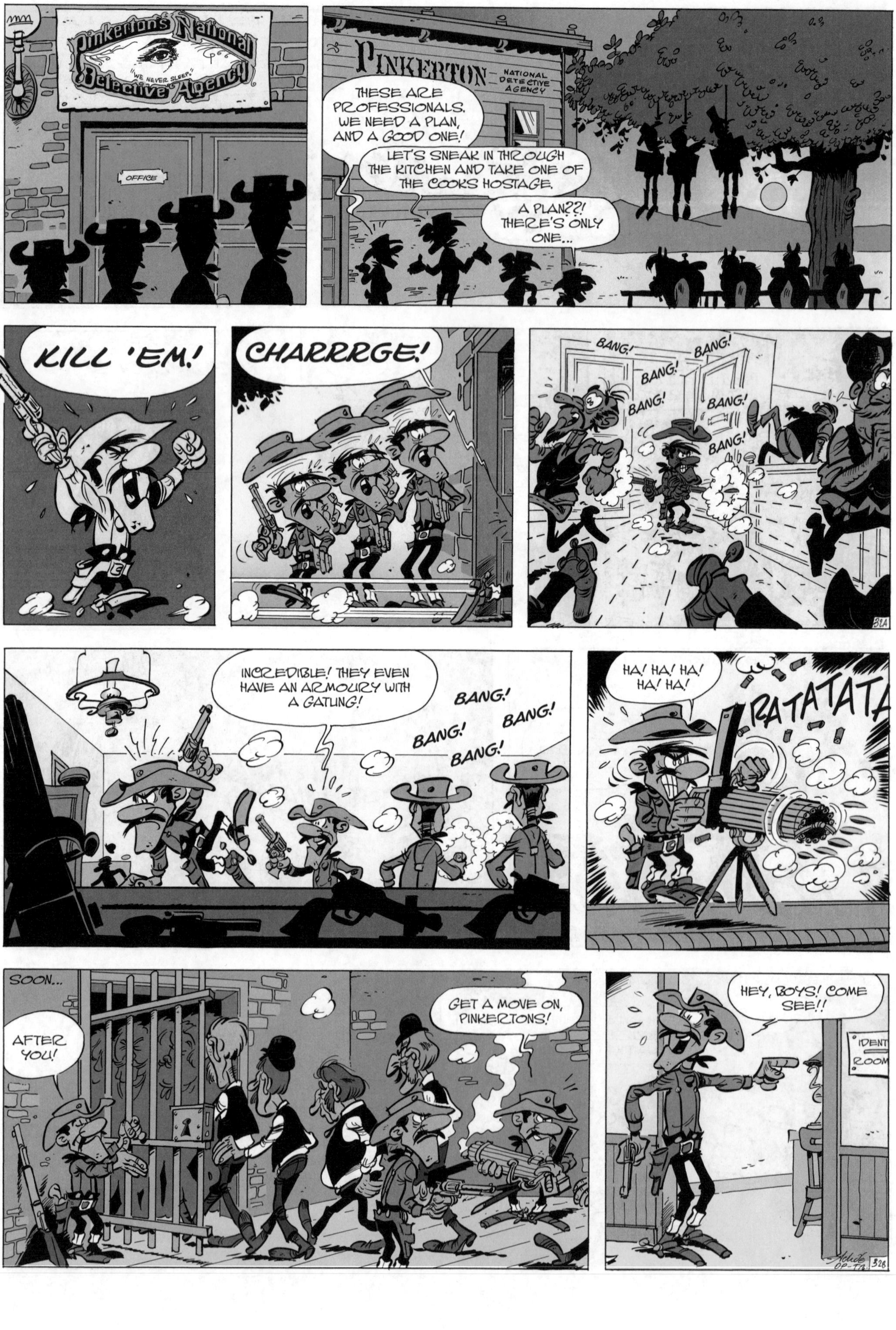

Pinkerton's National Detective Agency
"WE NEVER SLEEP."
OFFICE
PINKERTON
NATIONAL DETECTIVE AGENCY
THESE ARE PROFESSIONALS. WE NEED A PLAN, AND A GOOD ONE!
LET'S SNEAK IN THROUGH THE KITCHEN AND TAKE ONE OF THE COOKS HOSTAGE.
A PLAN??! THERE'S ONLY ONE...
KILL 'EM!
CHARRRGE!
BANG! BANG! BANG! BANG! BANG! BANG!
INCREDIBLE! THEY EVEN HAVE AN ARMOURY WITH A GATLING!
BANG! BANG! BANG! BANG!
HA! HA! HA! HA! HA!
RATATATA
SOON...
AFTER YOU!
GET A MOVE ON, PINKERTONS!
HEY, BOYS! COME SEE!!
IDENT ROOM

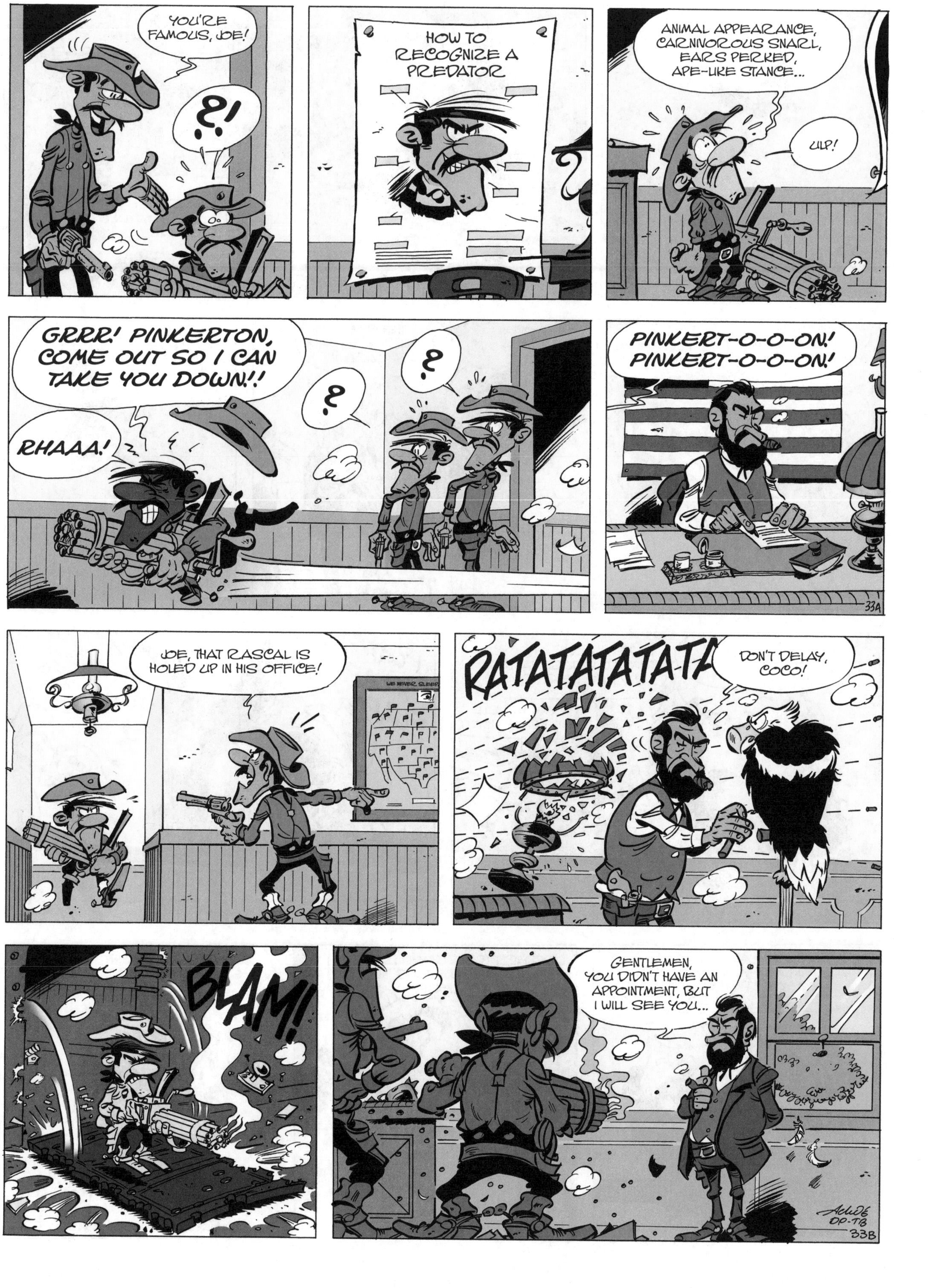
YOU'RE FAMOUS, JOE!
?!
HOW TO RECOGNIZE A PREDATOR
ANIMAL APPEARANCE, CARNIVOROUS SNARL, EARS PERKED, APE-LIKE STANCE...
ULP!
GRRR! PINKERTON, COME OUT SO I CAN TAKE YOU DOWN!!
RHAAA!
?
?
PINKERT-O-O-ON! PINKERT-O-O-ON!
33A
JOE, THAT RASCAL IS HOLED UP IN HIS OFFICE!
WE NEVER SLEEP
RATATATATATATA
DON'T DELAY, COCO!
BLAM!
GENTLEMEN, YOU DIDN'T HAVE AN APPOINTMENT, BUT I WILL SEE YOU...
33B

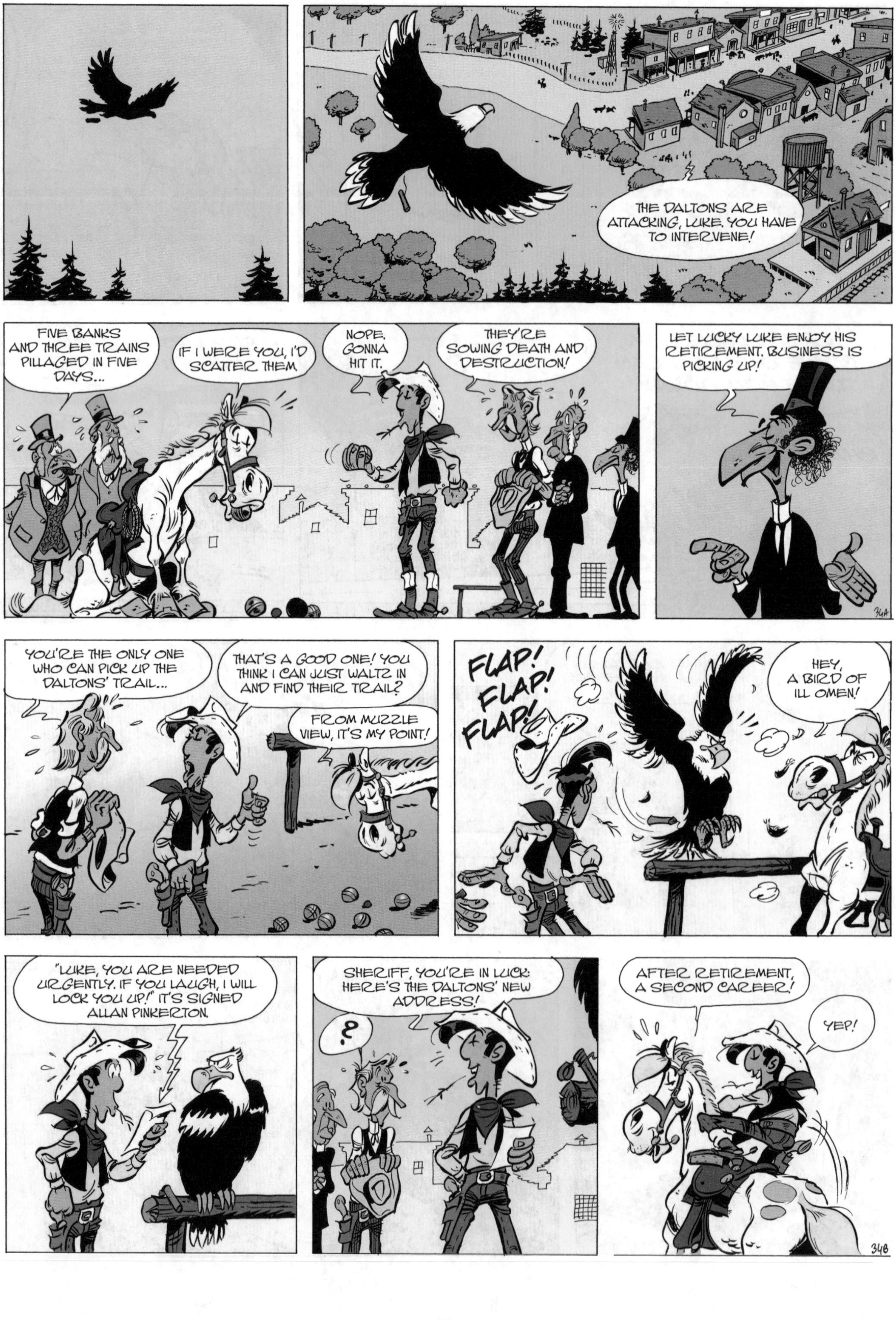
THE DALTONS ARE ATTACKING, LUKE. YOU HAVE TO INTERVENE!
FIVE BANKS AND THREE TRAINS PILLAGED IN FIVE DAYS...
IF I WERE YOU, I'D SCATTER THEM
NOPE. GONNA HIT IT.
THEY'RE SOWING DEATH AND DESTRUCTION!
LET LUCKY LUKE ENJOY HIS RETIREMENT. BUSINESS IS PICKING UP!
34A
YOU'RE THE ONLY ONE WHO CAN PICK UP THE DALTONS' TRAIL...
THAT'S A GOOD ONE! YOU THINK I CAN JUST WALTZ IN AND FIND THEIR TRAIL?
FROM MUZZLE VIEW, IT'S MY POINT!
FLAP! FLAP! FLAP!
HEY, A BIRD OF ILL OMEN!
"LUKE, YOU ARE NEEDED URGENTLY. IF YOU LAUGH, I WILL LOCK YOU UP!" IT'S SIGNED ALLAN PINKERTON.
SHERIFF, YOU'RE IN LUCK: HERE'S THE DALTONS' NEW ADDRESS!
?
AFTER RETIREMENT, A SECOND CAREER!
YEP!
34B

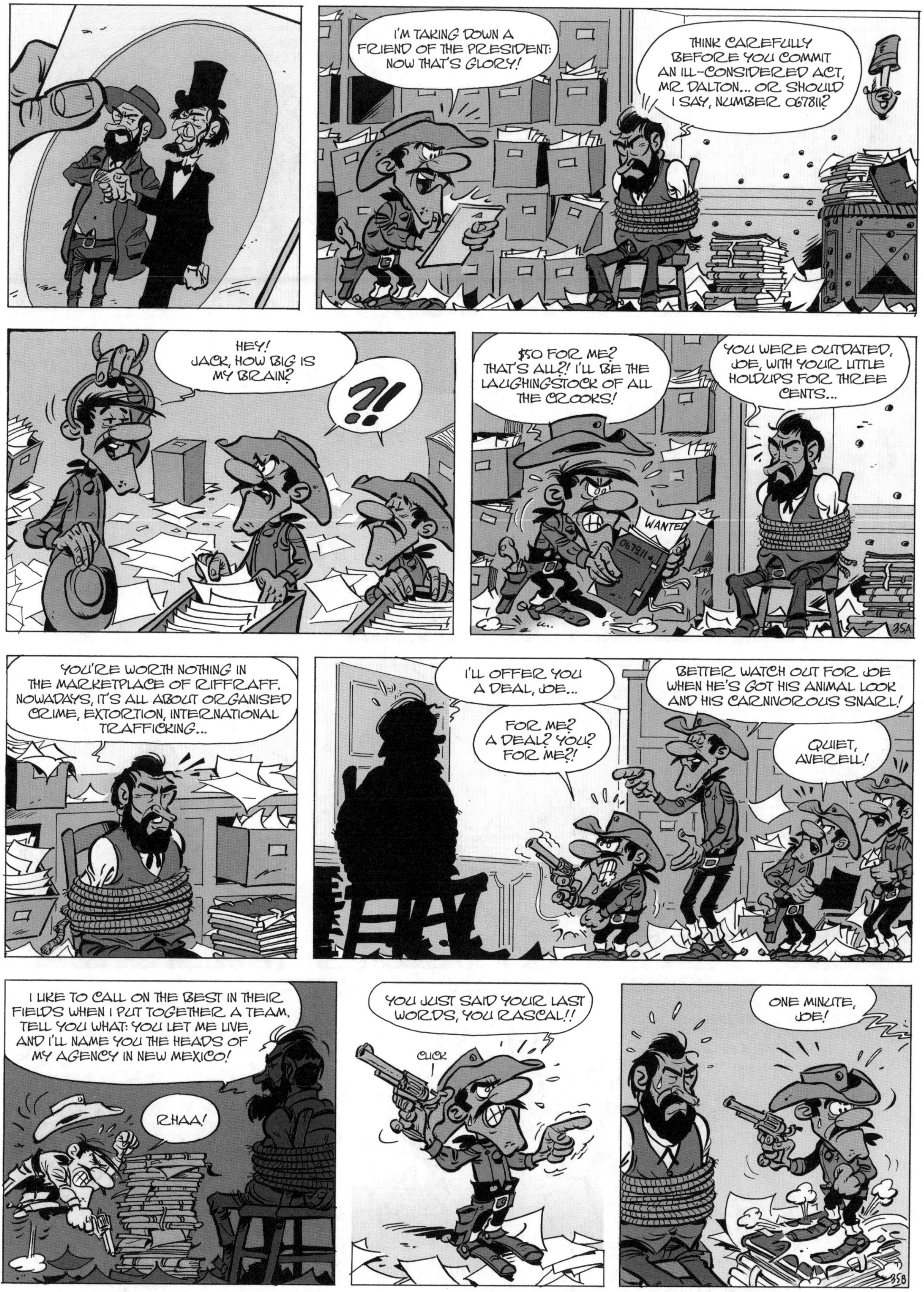
I'M TAKING DOWN A FRIEND OF THE PRESIDENT: NOW THAT'S GLORY!
THINK CAREFULLY BEFORE YOU COMMIT AN ILL-CONSIDERED ACT, MR DALTON... OR SHOULD I SAY, NUMBER 067811?
HEY! JACK, HOW BIG IS MY BRAIN?
?!!
$50 FOR ME? THAT'S ALL?! I'LL BE THE LAUGHINGSTOCK OF ALL THE CROOKS!
YOU WERE OUTDATED, JOE, WITH YOUR LITTLE HOLDUPS FOR THREE CENTS...
WANTED
YOU'RE WORTH NOTHING IN THE MARKETPLACE OF RIFFRAFF. NOWADAYS, IT'S ALL ABOUT ORGANISED CRIME, EXTORTION, INTERNATIONAL TRAFFICKING...
I'LL OFFER YOU A DEAL, JOE...
FOR ME? A DEAL? YOU? FOR ME?!
BETTER WATCH OUT FOR JOE WHEN HE'S GOT HIS ANIMAL LOOK AND HIS CARNIVOROUS SNARL!
QUIET, AVERELL!
I LIKE TO CALL ON THE BEST IN THEIR FIELDS WHEN I PUT TOGETHER A TEAM. TELL YOU WHAT: YOU LET ME LIVE, AND I'LL NAME YOU THE HEADS OF MY AGENCY IN NEW MEXICO!
RHAA!
YOU JUST SAID YOUR LAST WORDS, YOU RASCAL!!
CLICK
ONE MINUTE, JOE!

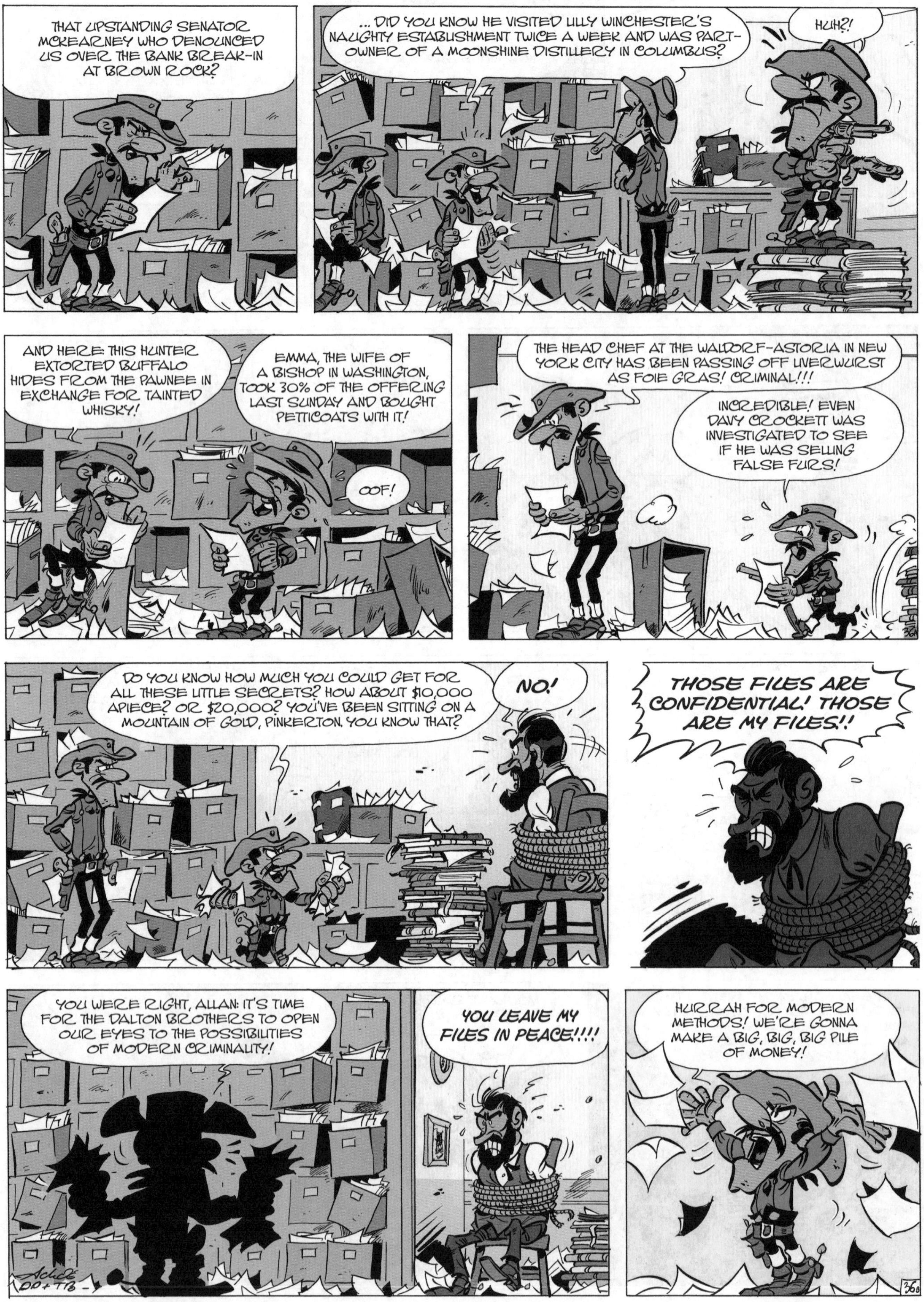
THAT UPSTANDING SENATOR MCKEARNEY WHO DENOUNCED US OVER THE BANK BREAK-IN AT BROWN ROCK?
... DID YOU KNOW HE VISITED LILLY WINCHESTER'S NAUGHTY ESTABLISHMENT TWICE A WEEK AND WAS PART-OWNER OF A MOONSHINE DISTILLERY IN COLUMBUS?
HUH?!
AND HERE: THIS HUNTER EXTORTED BUFFALO HIDES FROM THE PAWNEE IN EXCHANGE FOR TAINTED WHISKY!
EMMA, THE WIFE OF A BISHOP IN WASHINGTON, TOOK 30% OF THE OFFERING LAST SUNDAY AND BOUGHT PETTICOATS WITH IT!
OOF!
THE HEAD CHEF AT THE WALDORF-ASTORIA IN NEW YORK CITY HAS BEEN PASSING OFF LIVERWURST AS FOIE GRAS! CRIMINAL!!!
INCREDIBLE! EVEN DAVY CROCKETT WAS INVESTIGATED TO SEE IF HE WAS SELLING FALSE FURS!
DO YOU KNOW HOW MUCH YOU COULD GET FOR ALL THESE LITTLE SECRETS? HOW ABOUT $10,000 APIECE? OR $20,000? YOU'VE BEEN SITTING ON A MOUNTAIN OF GOLD, PINKERTON. YOU KNOW THAT?
NO!
THOSE FILES ARE CONFIDENTIAL! THOSE ARE MY FILES!!
YOU WERE RIGHT, ALLAN: IT'S TIME FOR THE DALTON BROTHERS TO OPEN OUR EYES TO THE POSSIBILITIES OF MODERN CRIMINALITY!
YOU LEAVE MY FILES IN PEACE!!!!
HURRAH FOR MODERN METHODS! WE'RE GONNA MAKE A BIG, BIG, BIG PILE OF MONEY!

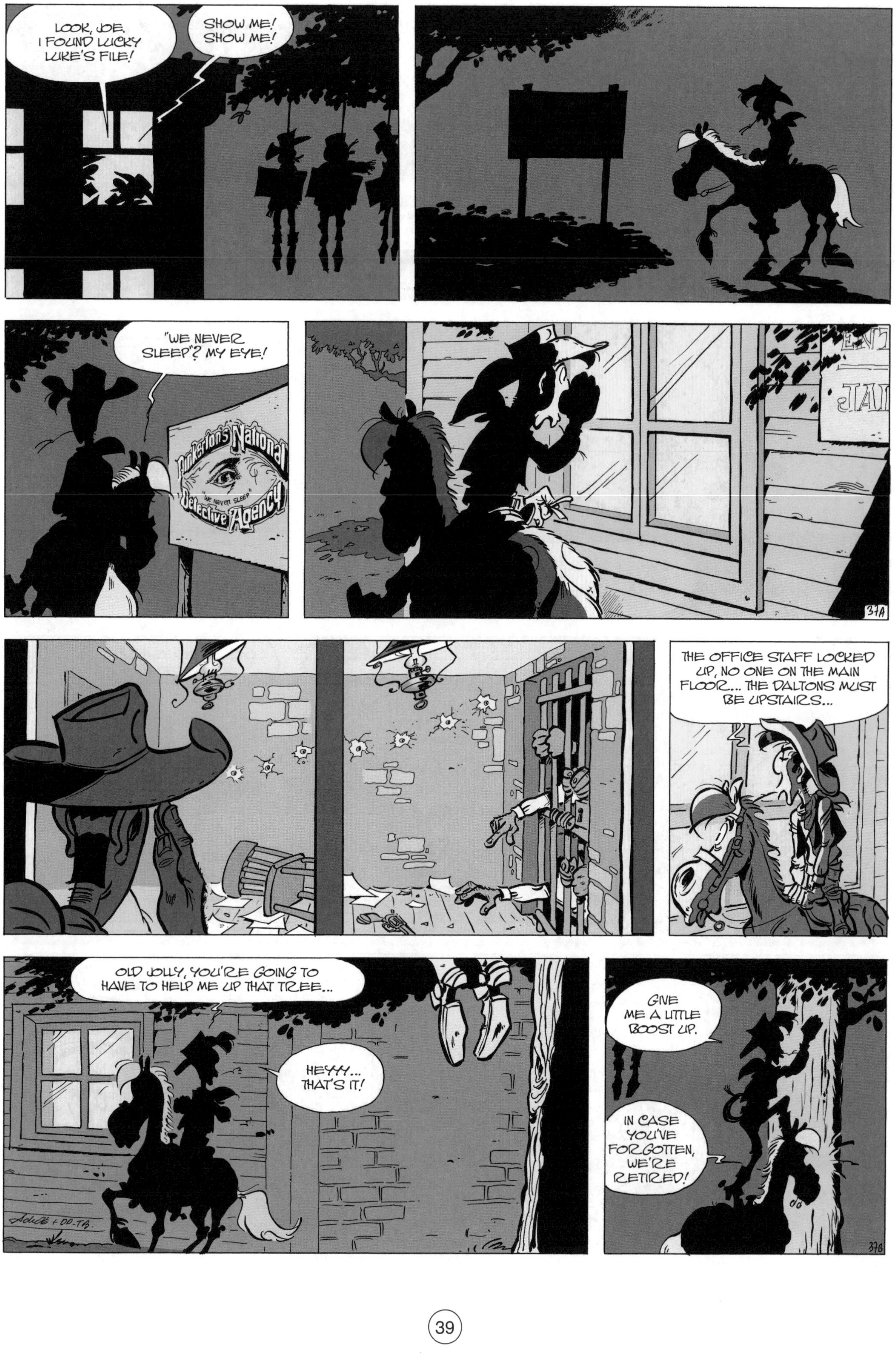
LOOK, JOE. I FOUND LUCKY LUKE'S FILE!
SHOW ME! SHOW ME!
"WE NEVER SLEEP"? MY EYE!
Pinkerton's National Detective Agency
"WE NEVER SLEEP"
THE OFFICE STAFF LOCKED UP, NO ONE ON THE MAIN FLOOR... THE DALTONS MUST BE UPSTAIRS...
OLD JOLLY, YOU'RE GOING TO HAVE TO HELP ME UP THAT TREE...
HEYYY... THAT'S IT!
GIVE ME A LITTLE BOOST UP.
IN CASE YOU'VE FORGOTTEN, WE'RE RETIRED!

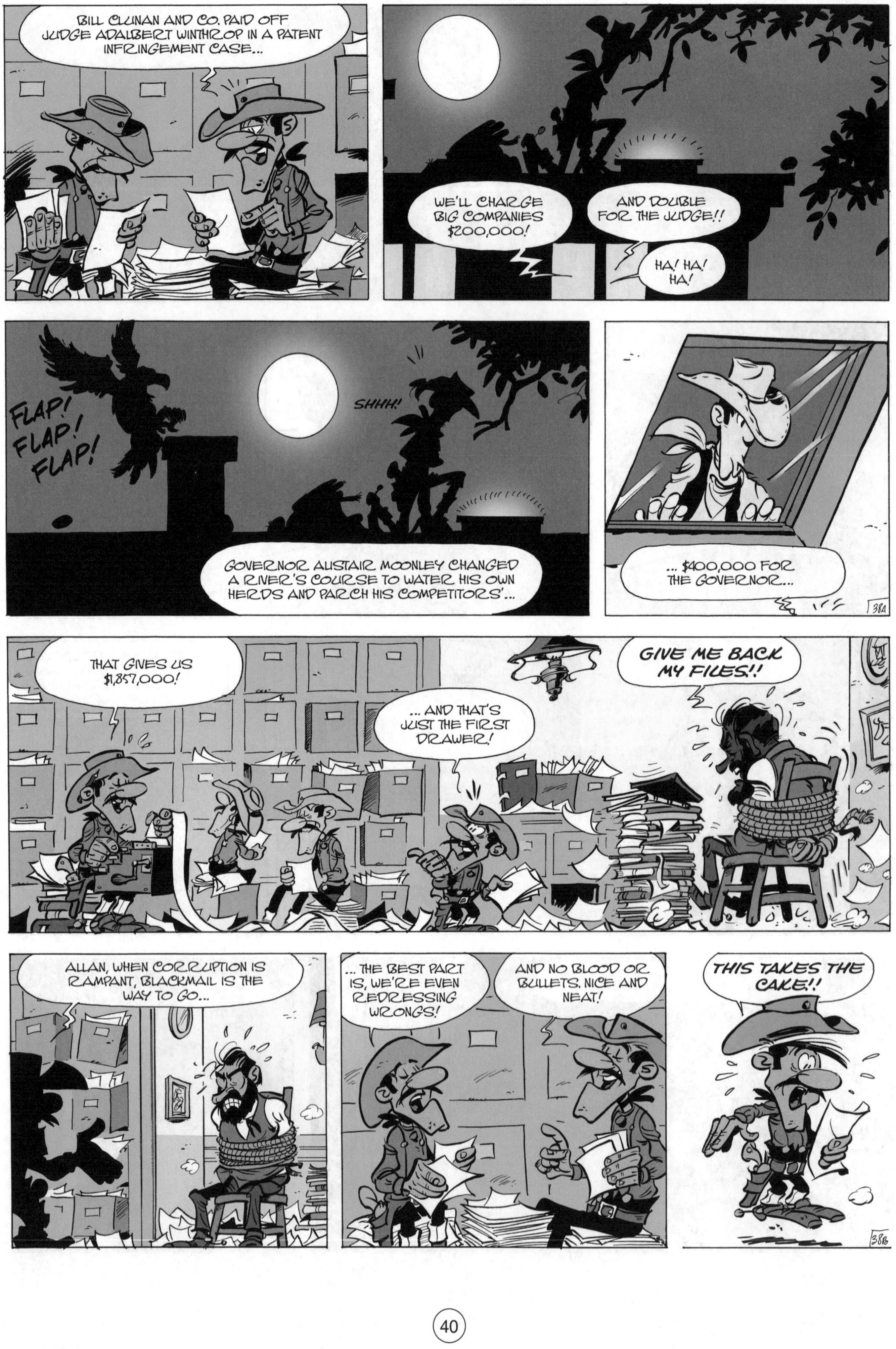
BILL CLUNAN AND CO. PAID OFF JUDGE ADALBERT WINTHROP IN A PATENT INFRINGEMENT CASE...
WE'LL CHARGE BIG COMPANIES $200,000!
AND DOUBLE FOR THE JUDGE!!
HA! HA! HA!
FLAP! FLAP! FLAP!
SHHH!
GOVERNOR ALISTAIR MOONLEY CHANGED A RIVER'S COURSE TO WATER HIS OWN HERDS AND PARCH HIS COMPETITORS'...
... $400,000 FOR THE GOVERNOR...
38A
THAT GIVES US $1,857,000!
... AND THAT'S JUST THE FIRST DRAWER!
GIVE ME BACK MY FILES!!
ALLAN, WHEN CORRUPTION IS RAMPANT, BLACKMAIL IS THE WAY TO GO...
... THE BEST PART IS, WE'RE EVEN REDRESSING WRONGS!
AND NO BLOOD OR BULLETS. NICE AND NEAT!
THIS TAKES THE CAKE!!
38B

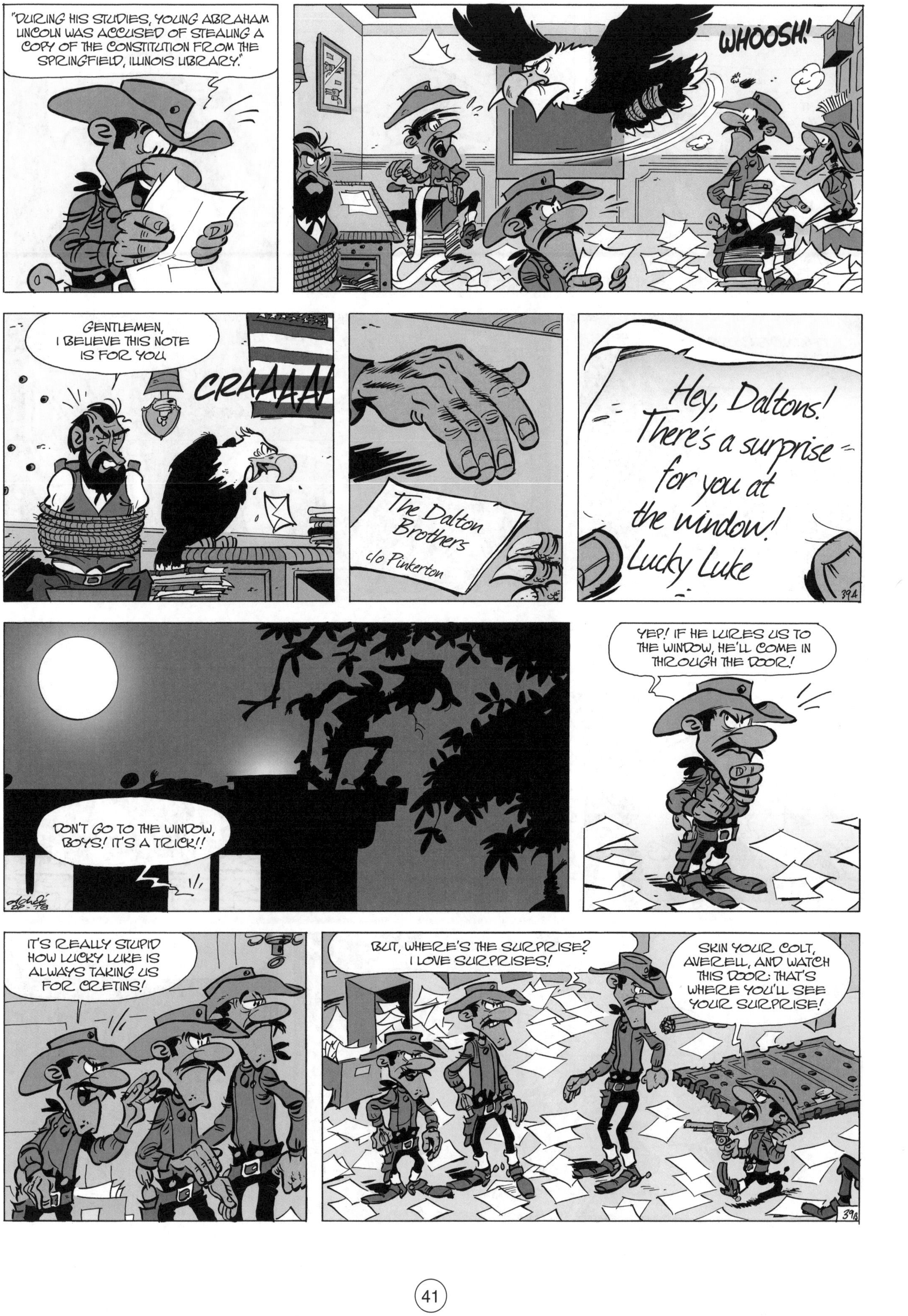

"DURING HIS STUDIES, YOUNG ABRAHAM LINCOLN WAS ACCUSED OF STEALING A COPY OF THE CONSTITUTION FROM THE SPRINGFIELD, ILLINOIS LIBRARY."
WHOOSH!
GENTLEMEN, I BELIEVE THIS NOTE IS FOR YOU
CRAAAAN
The Dalton Brothers c/o Pinkerton
Hey, Daltons! There's a surprise for you at the window! Lucky Luke
DON'T GO TO THE WINDOW, BOYS! IT'S A TRICK!!
YEP! IF HE LURES US TO THE WINDOW, HE'LL COME IN THROUGH THE DOOR!
IT'S REALLY STUPID HOW LUCKY LUKE IS ALWAYS TAKING US FOR CRETINS!
BUT, WHERE'S THE SURPRISE? I LOVE SURPRISES!
SKIN YOUR COLT, AVERELL, AND WATCH THIS DOOR: THAT'S WHERE YOU'LL SEE YOUR SURPRISE!

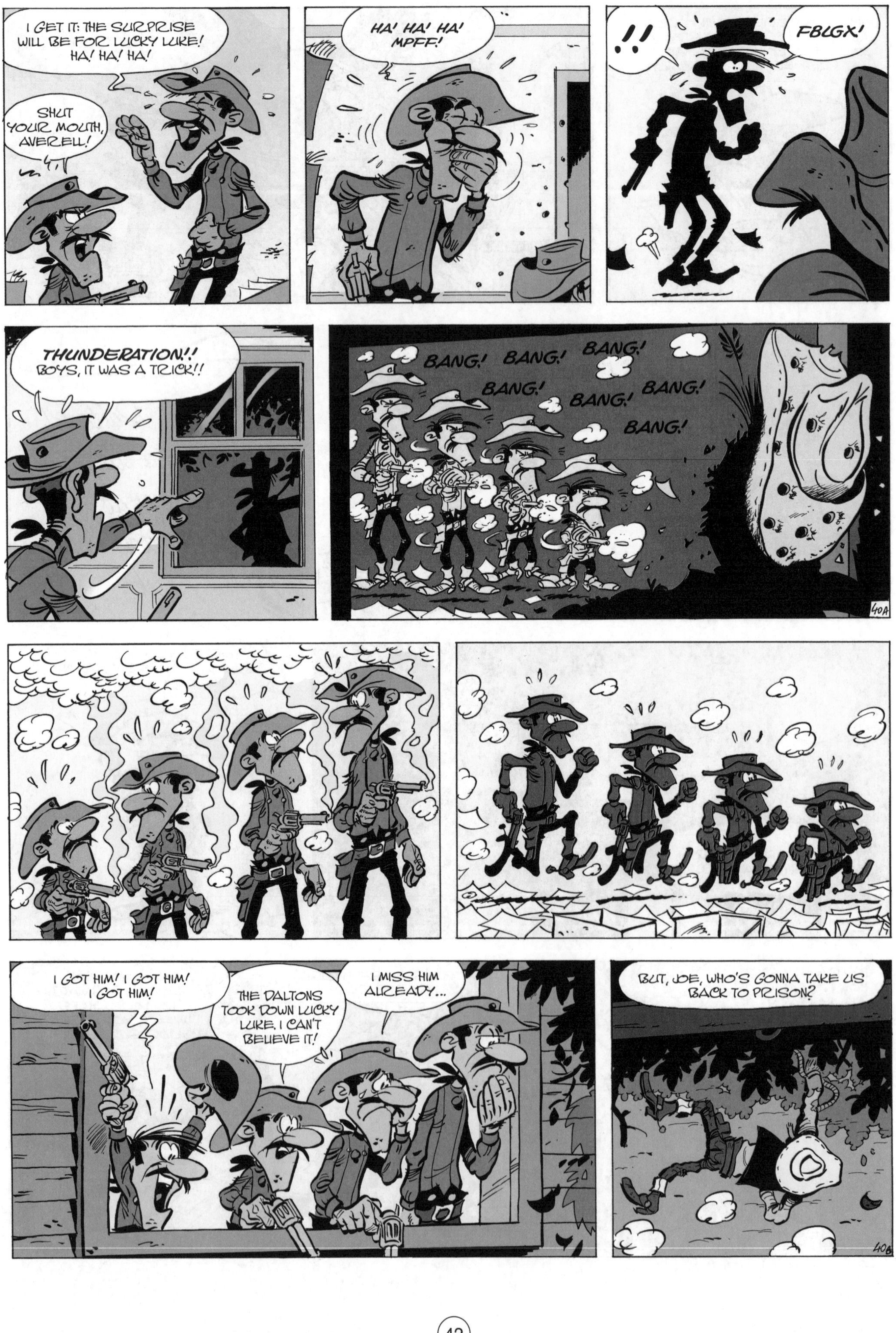

I GET IT: THE SURPRISE WILL BE FOR LUCKY LUKE! HA! HA! HA!
SHUT YOUR MOUTH, AVERELL!
HA! HA! HA! MPFF!
!!
FBLGX!
THUNDERATION!! BOYS, IT WAS A TRICK!!
BANG! BANG! BANG!
BANG! BANG! BANG!
BANG!
I GOT HIM! I GOT HIM! I GOT HIM!
THE DALTONS TOOK DOWN LUCKY LUKE. I CAN'T BELIEVE IT!
I MISS HIM ALREADY...
BUT, JOE, WHO'S GONNA TAKE US BACK TO PRISON?

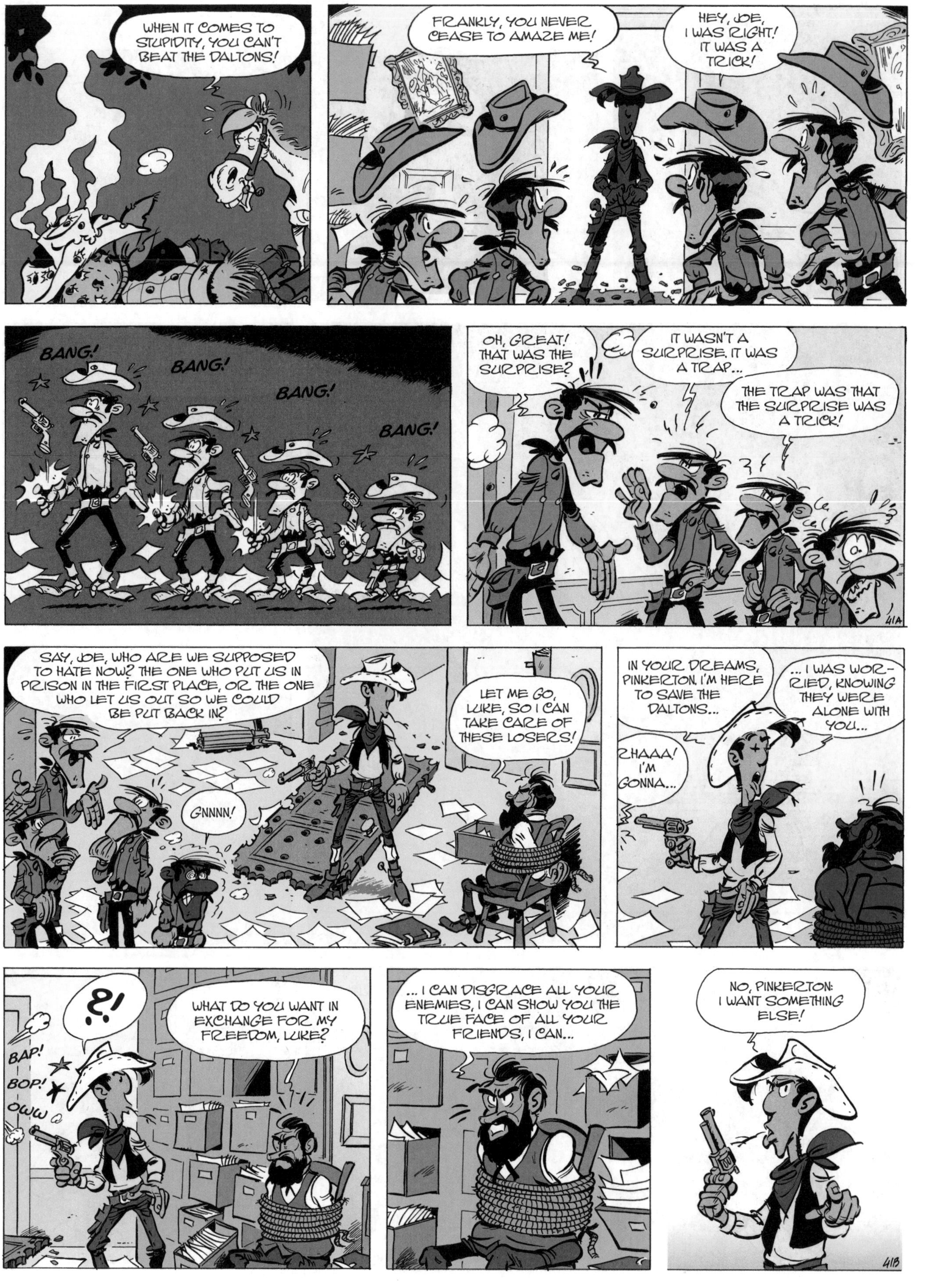
WHEN IT COMES TO STUPIDITY, YOU CAN'T BEAT THE DALTONS!
FRANKLY, YOU NEVER CEASE TO AMAZE ME!
HEY, JOE, I WAS RIGHT! IT WAS A TRICK!
BANG!
BANG!
BANG!
BANG!
OH, GREAT! THAT WAS THE SURPRISE?
IT WASN'T A SURPRISE. IT WAS A TRAP...
THE TRAP WAS THAT THE SURPRISE WAS A TRICK!
41A
SAY, JOE, WHO ARE WE SUPPOSED TO HATE NOW? THE ONE WHO PUT US IN PRISON IN THE FIRST PLACE, OR THE ONE WHO LET US OUT SO WE COULD BE PUT BACK IN?
GNNNN!
LET ME GO, LUKE, SO I CAN TAKE CARE OF THESE LOSERS!
IN YOUR DREAMS, PINKERTON. I'M HERE TO SAVE THE DALTONS...
... I WAS WORRIED, KNOWING THEY WERE ALONE WITH YOU...
RHAAA! I'M GONNA...
?!
BAP!
BOP!
OWW
WHAT DO YOU WANT IN EXCHANGE FOR MY FREEDOM, LUKE?
... I CAN DISGRACE ALL YOUR ENEMIES, I CAN SHOW YOU THE TRUE FACE OF ALL YOUR FRIENDS, I CAN...
NO, PINKERTON: I WANT SOMETHING ELSE!
41B

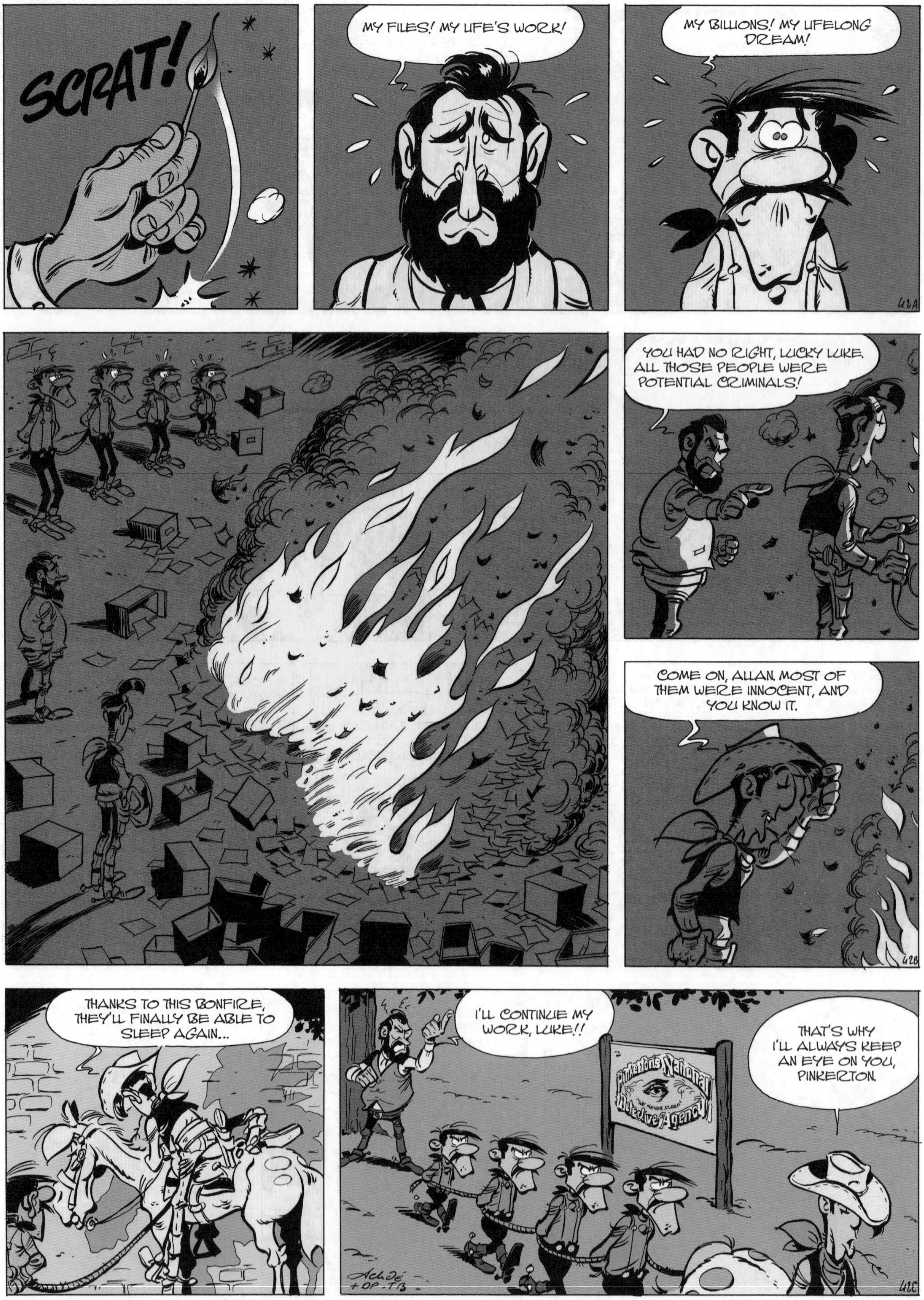
SCRAT!
MY FILES! MY LIFE'S WORK!
MY BILLIONS! MY LIFELONG DREAM!
YOU HAD NO RIGHT, LUCKY LUKE. ALL THOSE PEOPLE WERE POTENTIAL CRIMINALS!
COME ON, ALLAN. MOST OF THEM WERE INNOCENT, AND YOU KNOW IT.
THANKS TO THIS BONFIRE, THEY'LL FINALLY BE ABLE TO SLEEP AGAIN...
I'LL CONTINUE MY WORK, LUKE!!
Pinkerton's National
"We never sleep"
Detective Agency
THAT'S WHY I'LL ALWAYS KEEP AN EYE ON YOU, PINKERTON.

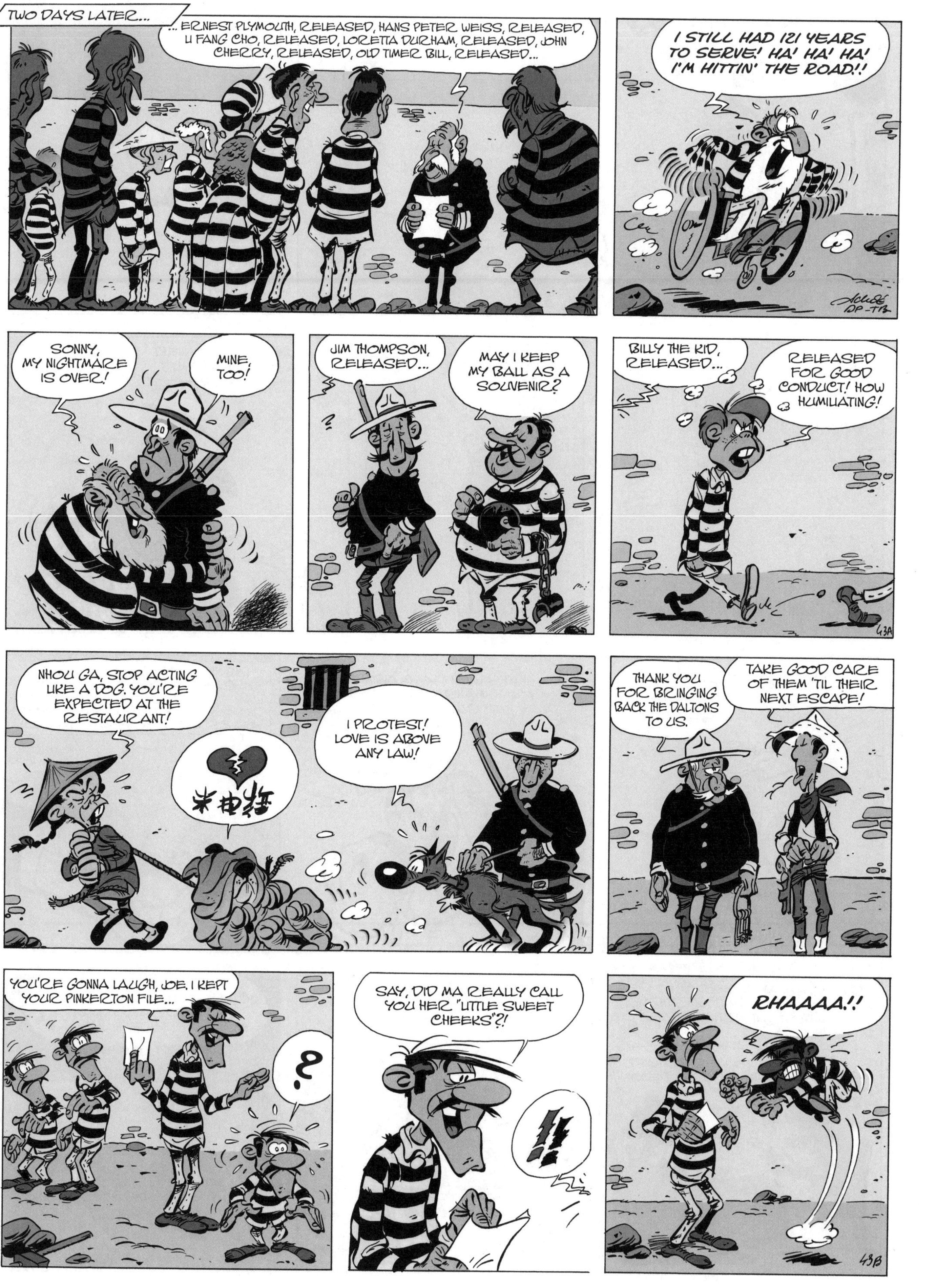
TWO DAYS LATER...
... ERNEST PLYMOUTH, RELEASED, HANS PETER WEISS, RELEASED, LI FANG CHO, RELEASED, LORETTA DURHAM, RELEASED, JOHN CHERRY, RELEASED, OLD TIMER BILL, RELEASED...
I STILL HAD 121 YEARS TO SERVE! HA! HA! HA! I'M HITTIN' THE ROAD!!
SONNY, MY NIGHTMARE IS OVER!
MINE, TOO!
JIM THOMPSON, RELEASED...
MAY I KEEP MY BALL AS A SOUVENIR?
BILLY THE KID, RELEASED...
RELEASED FOR GOOD CONDUCT! HOW HUMILIATING!
NHOU GA, STOP ACTING LIKE A DOG. YOU'RE EXPECTED AT THE RESTAURANT!
I PROTEST! LOVE IS ABOVE ANY LAW!
THANK YOU FOR BRINGING BACK THE DALTONS TO US.
TAKE GOOD CARE OF THEM 'TIL THEIR NEXT ESCAPE!
YOU'RE GONNA LAUGH, JOE. I KEPT YOUR PINKERTON FILE...
?
SAY, DID MA REALLY CALL YOU HER "LITTLE SWEET CHEEKS"?!
!!
RHAAAA!!

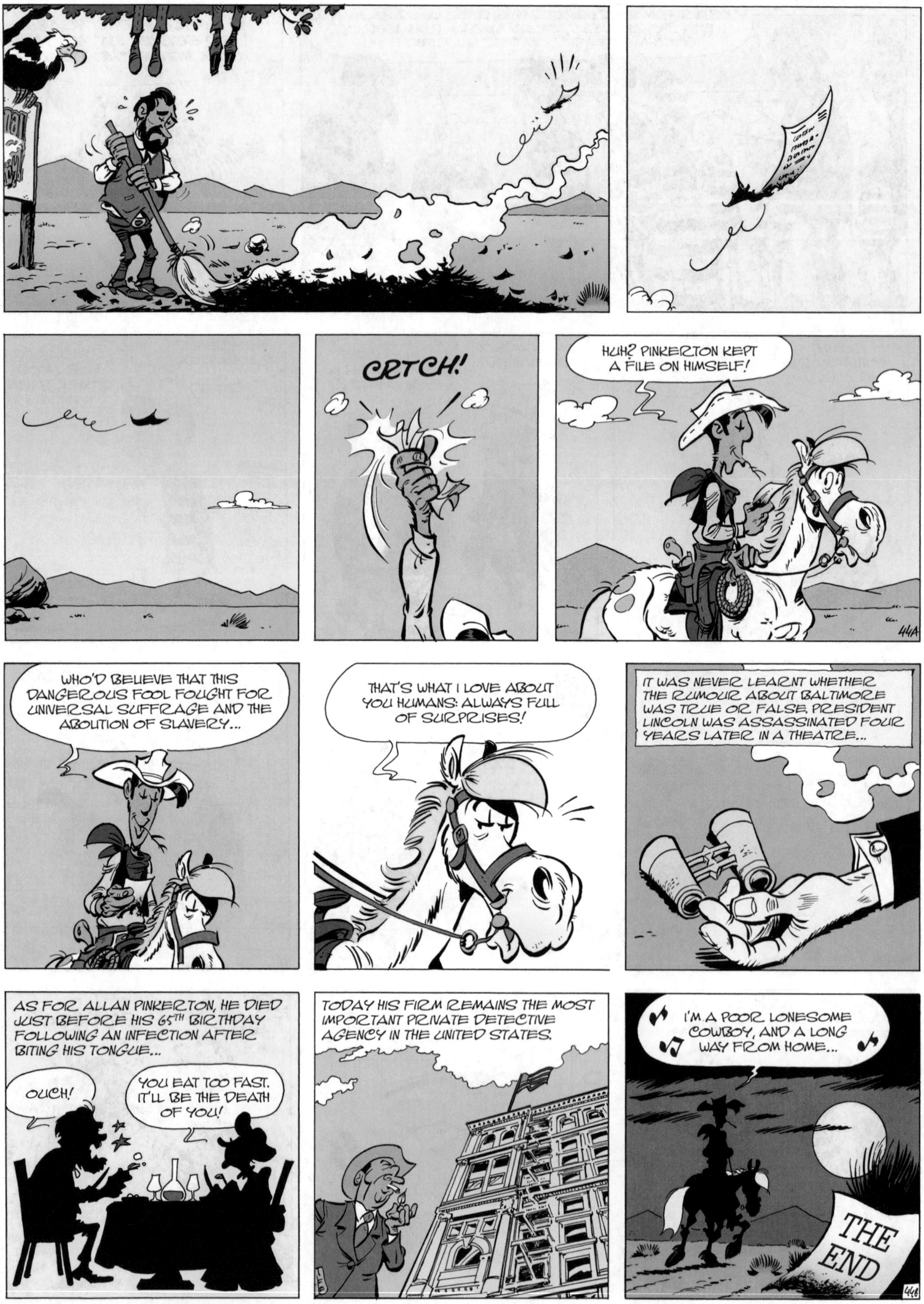
CRTCH!
HUH? PINKERTON KEPT A FILE ON HIMSELF!
WHO'D BELIEVE THAT THIS DANGEROUS FOOL FOUGHT FOR UNIVERSAL SUFFRAGE AND THE ABOLITION OF SLAVERY...
THAT'S WHAT I LOVE ABOUT YOU HUMANS: ALWAYS FULL OF SURPRISES!
IT WAS NEVER LEARNT WHETHER THE RUMOUR ABOUT BALTIMORE WAS TRUE OR FALSE. PRESIDENT LINCOLN WAS ASSASSINATED FOUR YEARS LATER IN A THEATRE...
AS FOR ALLAN PINKERTON, HE DIED JUST BEFORE HIS 65TH BIRTHDAY FOLLOWING AN INFECTION AFTER BITING HIS TONGUE...
OUCH!
YOU EAT TOO FAST. IT'LL BE THE DEATH OF YOU!
TODAY HIS FIRM REMAINS THE MOST IMPORTANT PRIVATE DETECTIVE AGENCY IN THE UNITED STATES.
I'M A POOR LONESOME COWBOY, AND A LONG WAY FROM HOME...
THE END

LUCKY LUKE

The man who shoots faster than his own shadow

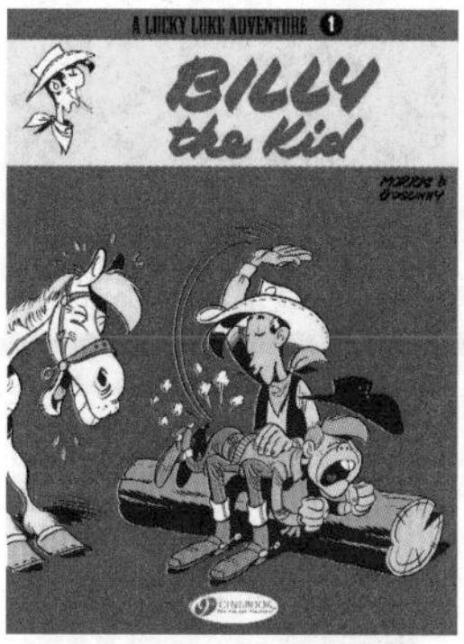
A LUCKY LUKE ADVENTURE 1
BILLY the Kid

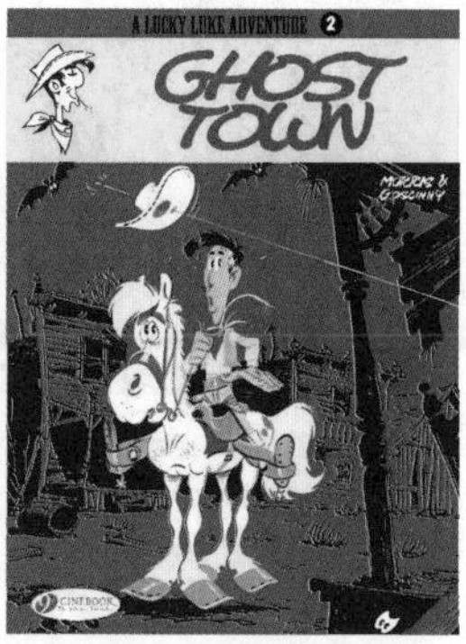
A LUCKY LUKE ADVENTURE 2
GHOST TOWN

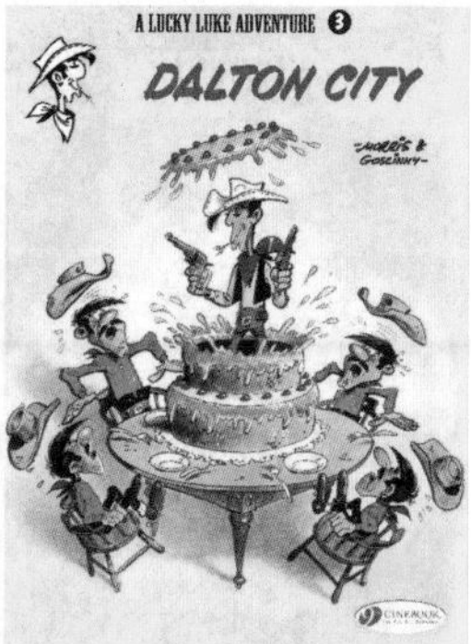
A LUCKY LUKE ADVENTURE 3
DALTON CITY

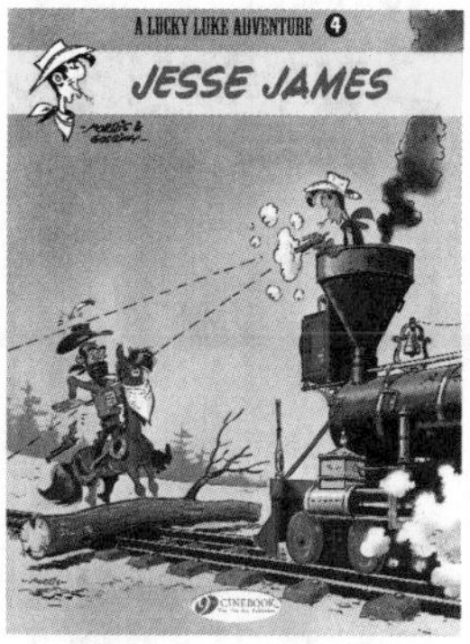
A LUCKY LUKE ADVENTURE 4
JESSE JAMES

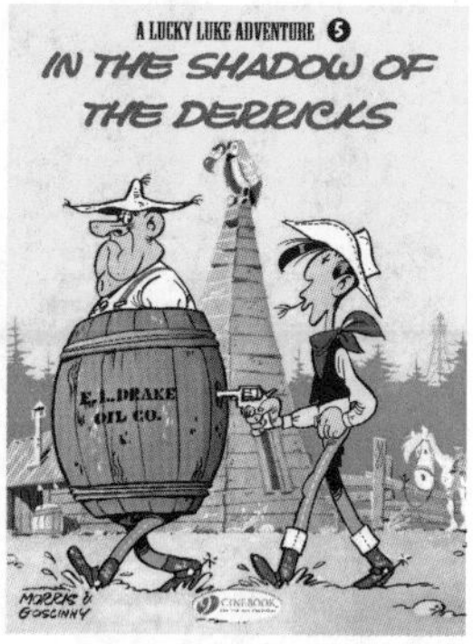
A LUCKY LUKE ADVENTURE 5
IN THE SHADOW OF THE DERRICKS
E. L. DRAKE OIL CO.

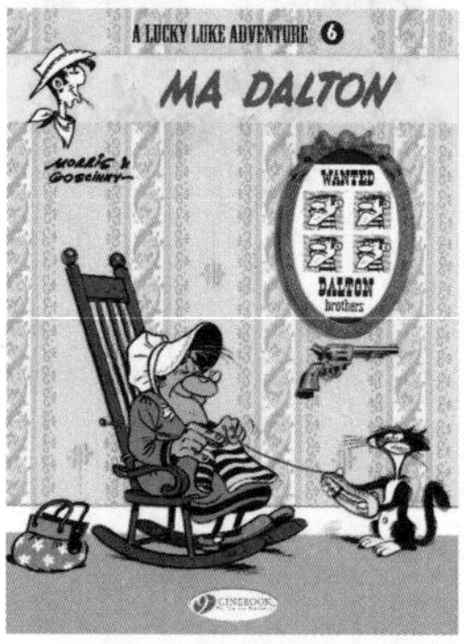
A LUCKY LUKE ADVENTURE 6
MA DALTON
WANTED
DALTON brothers

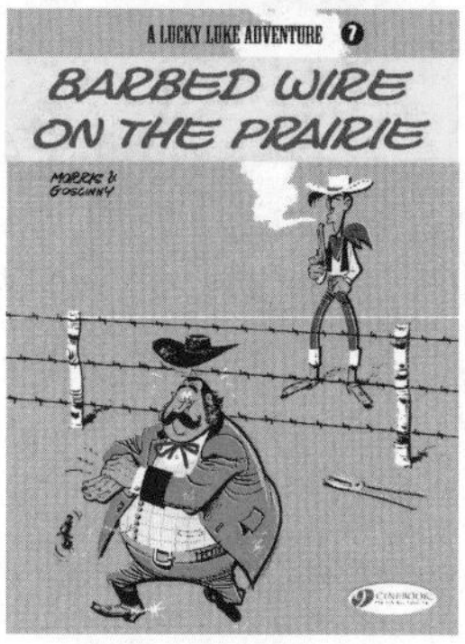
A LUCKY LUKE ADVENTURE 7
BARBED WIRE ON THE PRAIRIE

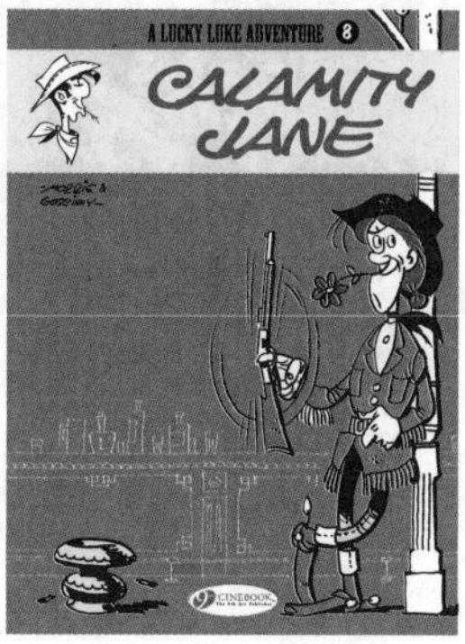
A LUCKY LUKE ADVENTURE 8
CALAMITY JANE

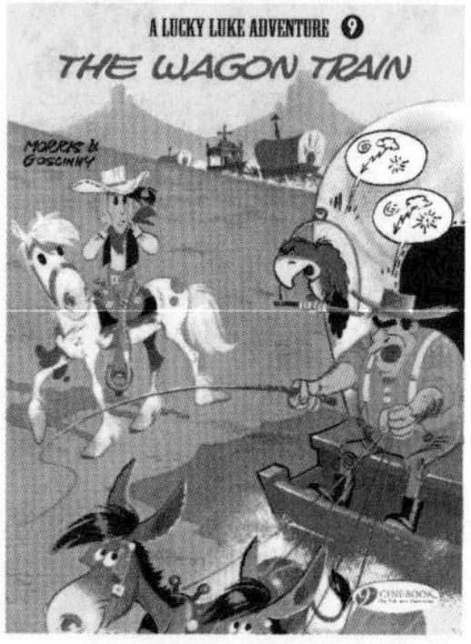
A LUCKY LUKE ADVENTURE 9
THE WAGON TRAIN

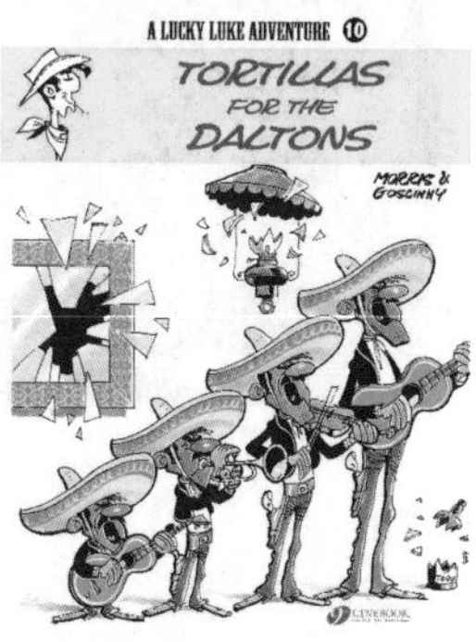
A LUCKY LUKE ADVENTURE 10
TORTILLAS FOR THE DALTONS

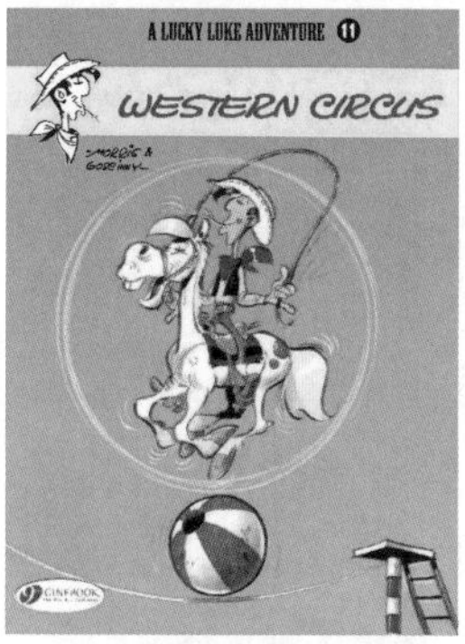
A LUCKY LUKE ADVENTURE 11
WESTERN CIRCUS

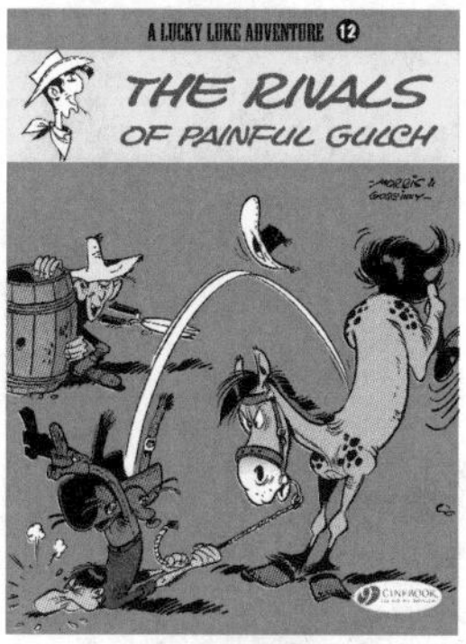
A LUCKY LUKE ADVENTURE 12
THE RIVALS OF PAINFUL GULCH

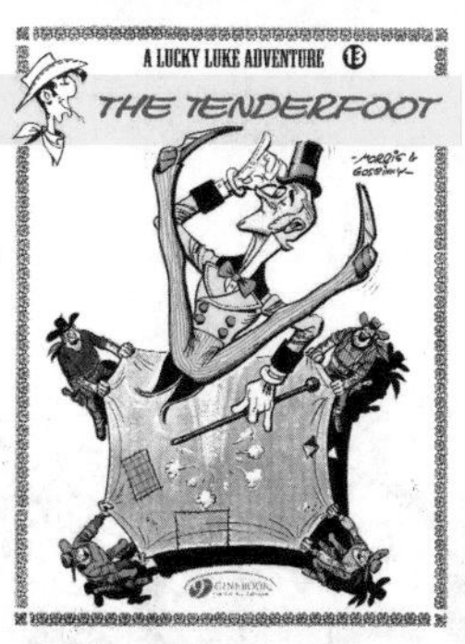
A LUCKY LUKE ADVENTURE 13
THE TENDERFOOT

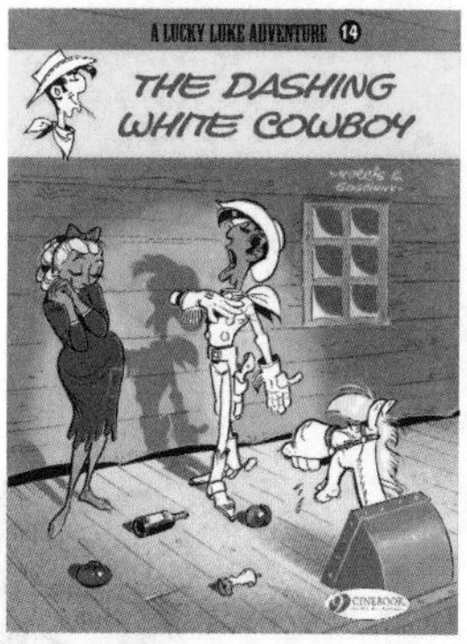
A LUCKY LUKE ADVENTURE 14
THE DASHING WHITE COWBOY

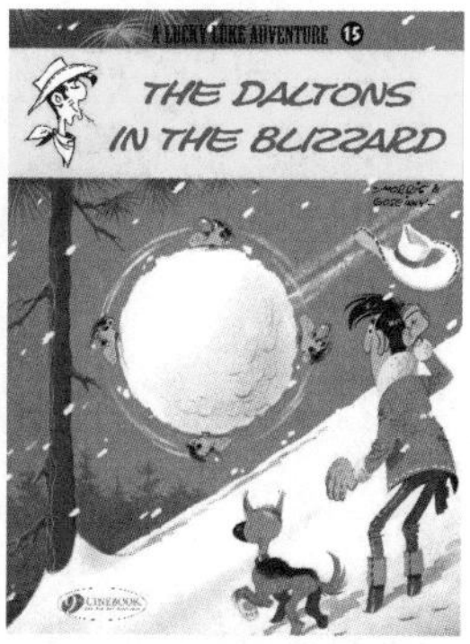
A LUCKY LUKE ADVENTURE 15
THE DALTONS IN THE BLIZZARD

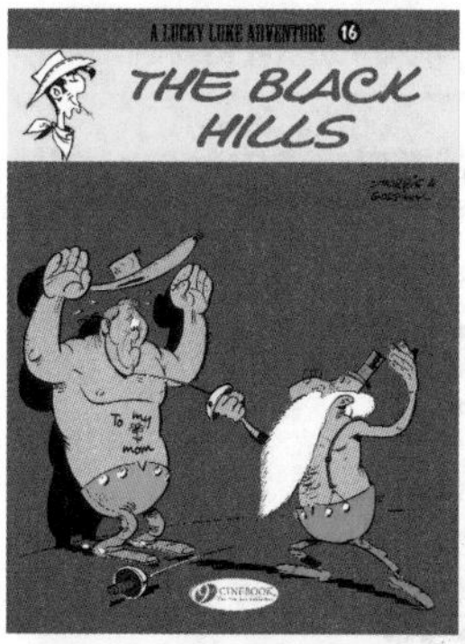
A LUCKY LUKE ADVENTURE 16
THE BLACK HILLS

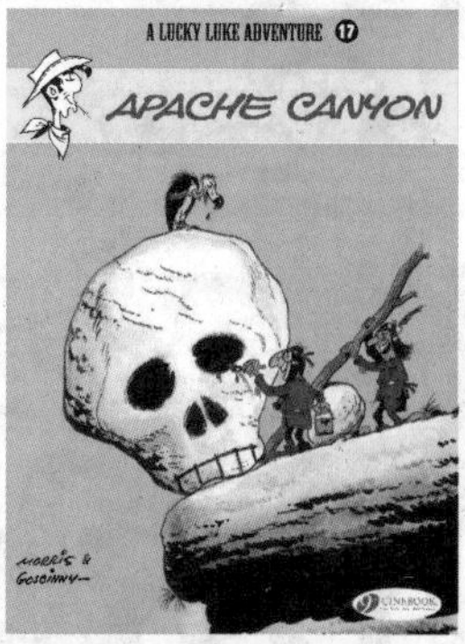
A LUCKY LUKE ADVENTURE 17
APACHE CANYON

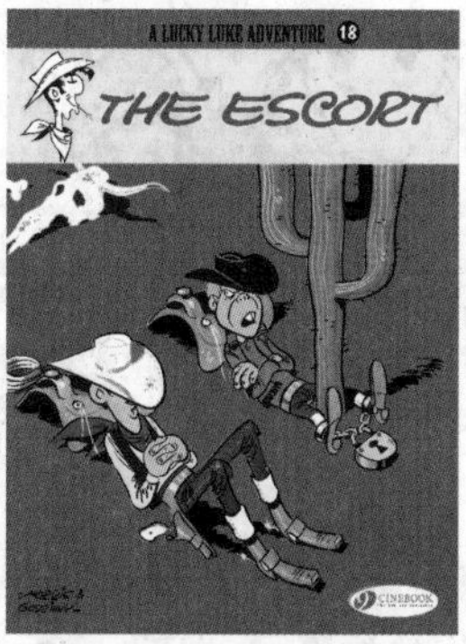
A LUCKY LUKE ADVENTURE 18
THE ESCORT

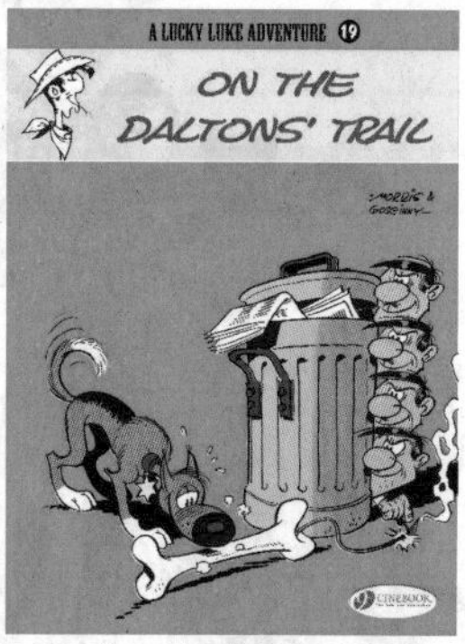
A LUCKY LUKE ADVENTURE 19
ON THE DALTONS' TRAIL

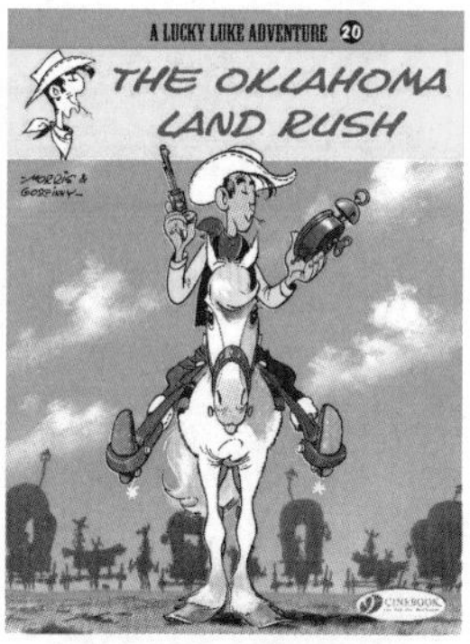
A LUCKY LUKE ADVENTURE 20
THE OKLAHOMA LAND RUSH

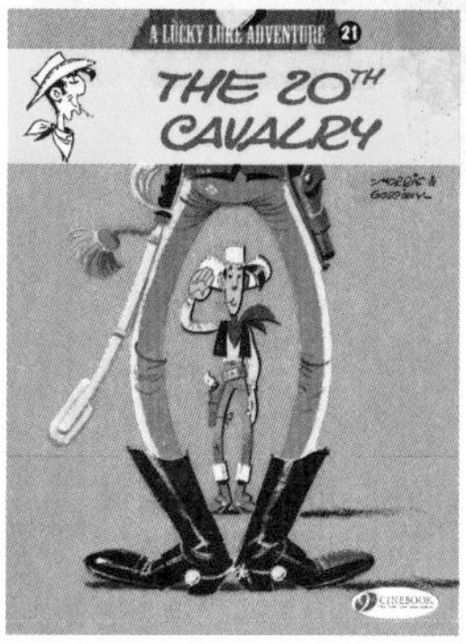
A LUCKY LUKE ADVENTURE 21
THE 20TH CAVALRY

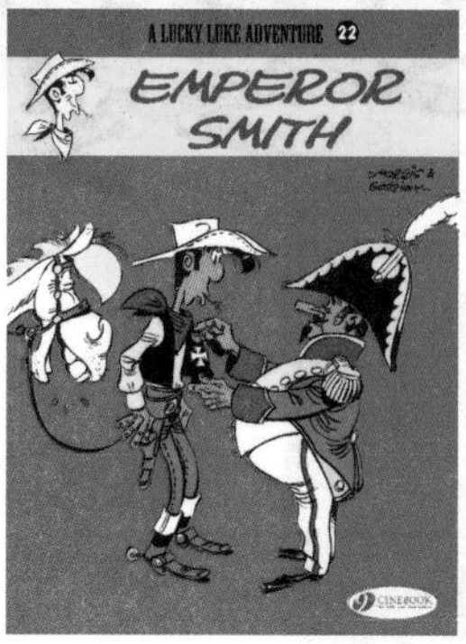
A LUCKY LUKE ADVENTURE 22
EMPEROR SMITH

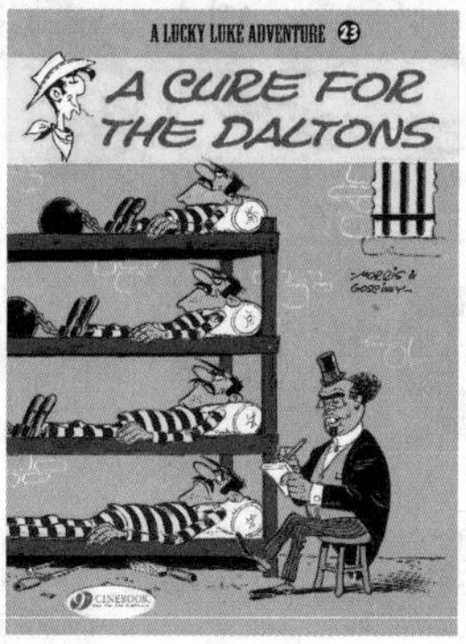
A LUCKY LUKE ADVENTURE 23
A CURE FOR THE DALTONS

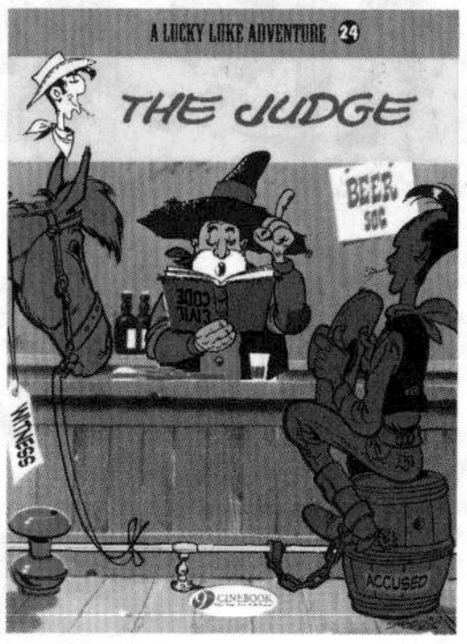
A LUCKY LUKE ADVENTURE 24
THE JUDGE
BEER 50¢
ACCUSED

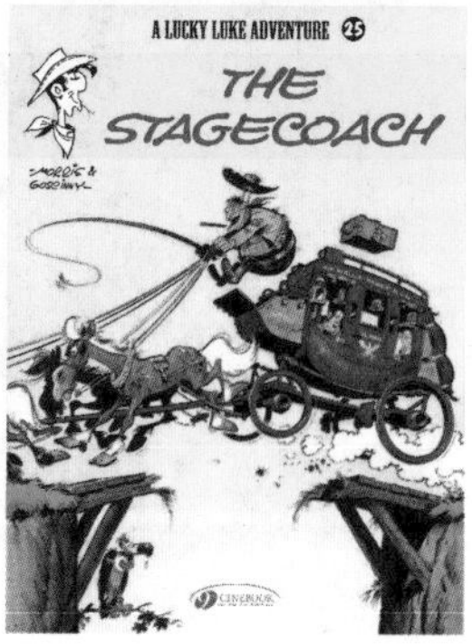
A LUCKY LUKE ADVENTURE 25
THE STAGECOACH

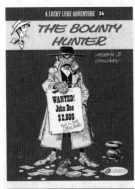

A LUCKY LUKE ADVENTURE 26
THE BOUNTY HUNTER
MORRIS & GOSCINNY
WANTED!
John Doe
$2,000
CINEBOOK

A LUCKY LUKE ADVENTURE 27
LUCKY LUKE
VERSUS JOSS JAMON
VOTE FOR
JOSS JAMON
CINEBOOK

A LUCKY LUKE ADVENTURE 28
THE DALTON COUSINS
SALOON
CINEBOOK

A LUCKY LUKE ADVENTURE 29
THE GRAND DUKE
CINEBOOK

A LUCKY LUKE ADVENTURE 30
THE DALTONS' ESCAPE
CINEBOOK

A LUCKY LUKE ADVENTURE 31
LUCKY LUKE
VERSUS THE PINKERTONS
CINEBOOK

A LUCKY LUKE ADVENTURE 32
RAILS ON THE PRAIRIE
CINEBOOK

DECEMBER 2011

A LUCKY LUKE ADVENTURE 33
THE ONE-ARMED BANDIT
CINEBOOK

FEBRUARY 2012

A LUCKY LUKE ADVENTURE 34
THE DALTONS
ALWAYS ON THE RUN
CINEBOOK

APRIL 2012

A LUCKY LUKE ADVENTURE 35
THE SINGING WIRE
CINEBOOK

JUNE 2012

MORRIS

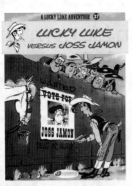

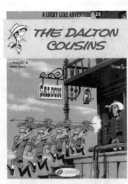

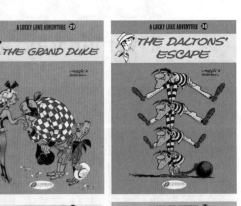

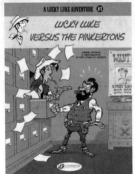

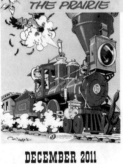

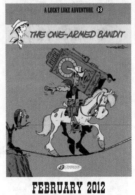

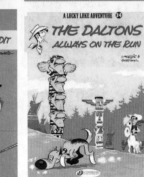

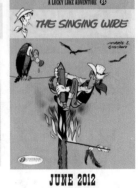

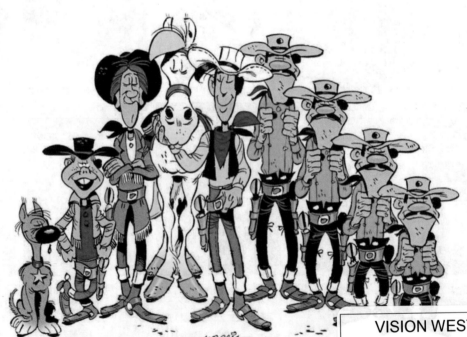

9th CINEBOOK
The 9th Art Publisher
www.cinebook.com